HUNG UP

ALSO BY KRISTEN TRACY

Lost It
Crimes of the Sarahs

HUNG UP

<3

♥♥♥?

UP

☺♥♥!!

<3

:)

KRISTEN TRACY

Simon Pulse

New York   London   Toronto   Sydney   New Delhi

𝅘𝅥 SIMON PULSE
An imprint of Simon & Schuster Children's Publishing Division
1230 Avenue of the Americas, New York, NY 10020
This Simon Pulse paperback edition March 2015
Text copyright © 2014 by Kristen Tracy
Cover photograph copyright © 2014 by Michael Frost
Cover illustrations copyright © 2014 by Mary Kate McDevitt
Also available in a Simon Pulse hardcover edition.
All rights reserved, including the right of reproduction in whole or in part in any form. SIMON PULSE and colophon are registered trademarks of Simon & Schuster, Inc. For information about special discounts for bulk purchases, please contact Simon & Schuster Special Sales at 1-866-506-1949 or business@simonandschuster.com. The Simon & Schuster Speakers Bureau can bring authors to your live event. For more information or to book an event contact the Simon & Schuster Speakers Bureau at 1-866-248-3049 or visit our website at www.simonspeakers.com.
Cover designed by Jessica Handelman
Interior designed by Mike Rosamilia
The text of this book was set in Scala OT.
Manufactured in the United States of America
2 4 6 8 10 9 7 5 3 1
The Library of Congress has cataloged the hardcover edition as follows:
Tracy, Kristen, 1972-
Hung up / Kristen Tracy. — First Simon Pulse hardcover edition.
pages cm
Summary: When a wrong number blossoms into a phone friendship for Lucy and James, two Vermont high school students, James wants to meet in person, but Lucy is strangely resistant. Told in the form of telephone calls and voice mail messages.
ISBN 978-1-4424-6075-1 (hardback) — ISBN 978-1-4424-6078-2 (ebook) — ISBN 978-1-4424-6077-5 (pbk)
[1. Friendship—Fiction. 2. Dating (Social customs)—Fiction.
3. Telephone calls—Fiction. 4. Vermont—Fiction.] I. Title.
PZ7.T68295Hu 2014 [Fic]—dc23   2013042272

To Brian Evenson,
for giving me the ultimate phone romance.

ACKNOWLEDGMENTS

I am deeply indebted to my agent, Sara Crowe, who once again found the perfect home for my story. Thanks to Anica Rissi for her expert advice and invaluable encouragement. And many thanks to Liesa Abrams for sweating all the details and shepherding this book into the world. Thank you, Bethany Buck, for all your kindness and support for this book and beyond. You've been there since *Lost It*, and that's a long time. I am very grateful for the entire team at Simon & Schuster for making my books be their very best. And special thanks to Stuart Dybek for telling stories that stick. Last of all thank you, Max, for contributing to this process by drooling on the keyboard, and to Brian, for mopping it up.

I know you like I know myself, I know you like the back of my hand, I know you like a book, I know you inside out. I know you like you'll never know.

—Gordon Lish, "The Merry Chase"

March 1, 11:25 a.m.

This is Lucy calling to update my order BKE-184. Looks like I won't need the leather strap after all. So, just to be clear, keep the rest of my order as is, but cancel the strap. Thanks!

March 5, 3:11 p.m.

It's Lucy again calling about my order BKE-184. Is it too late to rethink materials? In the end, recycled aluminum just sounds cheap. I'd rather go with the slate. All the reviews I've read say that slate will endure both heat and snow better. Plus, it has more effective results for tree attachment. Thanks for working with me. Can you please call me so I know you got this order change? My number is 802-555-0129.

March 6, 4:10 p.m.

It's Lucy. I called yesterday about order BKE-184. Nobody has gotten back to me. Please let me know that my order has been updated. Natural slate plaque. No leather strap.

March 8, 10:04 a.m.

It's Lucy calling about order BKE-184. I'd like confirmation that you received my requests for an order change. I'm worried because you still haven't called me back. I'm not high maintenance, if that's what you're thinking. I'm not going to modify anything beyond this point. I understand that you have strict shipping dates. If you're upset about my leather strap cancellation, just go ahead and ignore it. I'm willing to eat the cost on that. I really want to know when you plan to ship my order. I'd also like to remind you that I've already paid in full. So I deserve a return phone call. I mean, I don't like threatening people. But I also don't like being jerked around. My number is 802-555-0129. You better call it.

March 15, 11:38 a.m.

Lucy: This is the last message I'm going to leave before I call the Better Business Bureau—

James: I'm speaking. You're not leaving a message.

Lucy: When are you going to ship my order?

James: I'm not.

Lucy: You have to! I paid for it.

James: My name is James and you haven't paid *me* anything for anything.

Lucy: Not cool, James. I paid somebody in your company.

James: I don't own a company. You're about the thirtieth person who's—

Lucy: Do I have the wrong number?

James: Not exactly . . .

Lucy: This sounds like a total scumbag operation.

James: No. There is no *operation*. My name is James Rusher. I'm a senior at Burlington High School. I'm not connected to this plaque/trophy/crystal awards business in any way. It's my cell phone. I just got it. I took a recycled number. I guess I got a deadbeat trophy company. I'm sorry to tell you this, but I think they've gone out of business.

Lucy: That sucks. I mean, I can't believe this is happening.

James: Um . . . It's not exactly the end of the world.

Lucy: Easy for you to say. What are my options here? What am I supposed to do about my order?

James: I guess you order another slate plaque without a leather strap from a different company?

Lucy: You know, you could pretend to have some sympathy. I've been robbed.

James: You're right. I'm sorry. You sound nice. I feel bad you got taken. The guy who ran that business sounds terrible. He even ripped off people who'd ordered gravestones for their pets.

Lucy: Wow.

James: I hope somebody catches up with him and makes him pay all these people back.

Lucy: Yeah. Okay. Thanks. I'll let you go.

James: Lucy, I bet with enough effort you can find this guy. It's really hard for people to just totally disappear.

Lucy: Um. Yeah, I'm pretty busy, and I have zero interest in playing detective, James. I think I'm just going to accept that I got screwed.

James: Your call.

Lucy: Yeah. It is. Okay, good luck with midterms.

James: How do you know I've got midterms?

Lucy: You said you go to Burlington High.

James: Interesting. And do *you* go to Burlington High?

Lucy: No, I live in Montpelier. I have a friend who goes to Burlington High.

James: Who?

Lucy: I'm not going to tell you my friend's name. You're a stranger.

James: Is it your *boyfriend*?

Lucy: I'm going to hang up on you, James.

James: Don't hang up.

Lucy: Stop being obnoxious.

James: No promises there. It's how I'm built.

Lucy: Are you going to call back all the people who are leaving you messages about this company?

James: I don't have that kind of time.

Lucy: You don't feel obligated?

James: Why would I feel obligated?

Lucy: Well, they're calling you.

James: I've got midterms to study for, remember?

Lucy: Okay. I'll let you go, James.

James: You're fun to talk to. You can call me anytime.

Lucy: Thanks. But I'm probably not going to do that. Bye.

March 17, 4:18 p.m.
James: Hey, Lucy, it's James. You called me last week about your plaque and leather strap. I told my friend Jairo about your situation. He says he knows how to get that stuff wholesale. Shoot us the dimensions you want, and he thinks he can get you what you need. Let me know if this works for you.

March 19, 5:52 p.m.
James: Hey, Lucy, Jairo can't fill your order. He got hit in the head with a tree limb today. Don't worry. He'll be okay. We tried to start a company using the disgruntled client base of the deadbeat trophy company. Not the people with outstanding orders. Those people are out of luck. But we figured we'd take the new callers. And this woman needed us to measure her mailbox, because she wanted a new address plaque. And it was near a tree. And Jairo underestimated his

strength. And he shoved her quaking aspen. And a limb fell and totally nailed him. Looks like we won't be taking that job. Anyway, I've been doing some sleuthing, and I think I have the home phone number of the now-defunct trophy company. I've been giving it out to people who call me with outstanding orders. It makes me feel like a cross between a private investigator and Robin Hood. Also, I feel a little bit like a bounty hunter. But don't worry—I don't own any weapons. Except for baseball bats, hockey sticks, stuff like that. And I only use those to play sports. Hey, this is a long message. And it's starting to sound weird. Sorry.

March 20, 3:30 p.m.

Lucy: Hi, James, that's too bad about your friend's head. From what I hear, quaking aspens can be very brittle and unpredictable. Mature ones can crush a bystander to death. It happens all the time. Well, maybe not all the time. Yes, give me the deadbeat plaque maker's home phone number. Also, it surprises me a great deal that you (a) consider a hockey stick to be a lethal weapon, and (b) feel a little bit like a bounty hunter. Have you ever seen a bounty hunter? I have, on TV. They're usually overly tattooed and pretty rough looking. Plus, they have mullets and violent tendencies. Is there something you should tell me?

March 21, sent 4:39 p.m.
James: What are you doing?

March 21, sent 4:41 p.m.
Lucy: I don't text. Ever.

March 21, sent 4:43 p.m.
James: Why not?

March 21, sent 4:44 p.m.
Lucy: I just don't and I'm serious. I will never respond to a text again.

March 21, sent 4:45 p.m.
James: That's weird. Texting would be fun.

March 22, 3:00 p.m.
Lucy: Hello?

James: It's James. Do you have a pen? I've got the number of the former owner of the scumbag operation. He lives in New Jersey now.

Lucy: That figures.

James: Are you ready?

Lucy: I have a pen.

James: I almost texted you this information.

Lucy: I don't text.

James: You mentioned that. Why not?

Lucy: I just don't.

James: Are you technophobic?

Lucy: No.

James: Do you have a crappy data plan?

Lucy: I'm not in a jokey mood, James. Just give me the number. Please.

James: Fine. Here it is. It's 201-555-0127.

Lucy: I'll call him tomorrow. I'm on my way out the door.

James: Where are you going?

Lucy: To the mall.

James: You're such a girl.

Lucy: I'm going to buy a knife.

James: For cooking?

Lucy: Camping.

James: Sweet. A woman who likes the wilderness and blades.

Lucy: I find that response alarming.

James: I'm probably going to call you later.

Lucy: I'll probably answer if you do.

March 24, 9:44 p.m.
Lucy: Is this James?

James: Yes, and I'm stuck.

Lucy: Inside of something?

James: Yes, a take-home essay. I can't find my way out.

Lucy: It's late. Maybe you should go to bed and work on it in the morning.

James: It's due in the morning.

Lucy: James, James, James. It's like my mother always tells me—extreme procrastination oft leads to excessive caffeination.

James: Your mother uses the word "oft"?

Lucy: Not every day. If you'll be staying up all night, I suggest drinking coffee.

James: But I don't drink coffee.

Lucy: Religious reasons?

James: No, it messes up my stomach.

Lucy: Try tea.

James: I need answers. Can you help me?

Lucy: I'm not writing your essay for you.

James: I just want to talk about the topic. You can help me get my juices flowing.

Lucy: You are the first guy who's ever asked me point-blank to help him get his juices flowing.

James: I didn't mean it that way.

Lucy: Oh, I know. If I thought you meant it dirty, I would've hung up.

James: Don't hang up. Seriously, I need your help.

Lucy: You don't even know me. I could be an F student.

James: You're an A student. I can tell.

Lucy: How?

James: You know weird facts about aspen trees.

Lucy: Well, I have gotten some Bs in my life.

James: I bet they were math related.

Lucy: Wrong.

James: I can tell that you're smart. In addition to that, I'm desperate. Can I bounce a few things off you?

Lucy: Okay. What's your essay about?

James: I had my choice of writing about either Charlotte Perkins Gilman's "The Yellow Wallpaper" or Stephen Crane's "The Open Boat." I chose the latter.

Lucy: Yeah, that makes sense. It sounds more masculine. The Gilman piece is more about women's issues.

James: I wouldn't mind writing an essay about women's issues. I'm avoiding it for another reason altogether.

Lucy: What's that?

James: I hate the scene where the woman snaps. All

that crawling around on the floor. When people lose their minds, even in literature, it creeps me out.

Lucy: Good to know. Hey, I've never read Crane's story. So don't say anything that will spoil the ending.

James: I promise not to tell you the order in which all the characters die.

Lucy: That wasn't funny.

James: It was to me.

Lucy: Then you're easy.

James: I'll take that as a compliment. But enough about my sex life. Let's get to the essay. Crane's story is about four men adrift at sea in a small boat: a cook, an oiler, a correspondent, and an injured captain. The basic theme is man versus nature. My teacher wants me to write an essay that examines the psychology of one of the characters, and explore how his choices determine his fate.

Lucy: That story sounds sexist. There are no women on the boat? What about the cook?

James: No, the cook is a dude. And the story is based on the writer's real life story. Crane was on a ship that wrecked off the coast of Florida. So it's not so much that the story is sexist, it's that seafaring is sexist in general.

Lucy: Okay. Which guy did you choose?

James: I think I'm going to choose the sea, and examine how its force deprives the characters of the opportunity to make choices.

Lucy: So you're avoiding the question altogether. Is this strategy born out of late-night panic or a long-standing desire to challenge authority?

James: Neither. I think the question assumes that the characters have power over their lives, and I think the story sort of suggests that these four guys bobbing in the ocean are at the mercy of something that doesn't give a shit about them. It doesn't matter what they do. The sea will determine their fates. It doesn't matter what they choose.

Lucy: Seems fatalistic.

James: It's naturalistic. It's what Crane and lots of other writers of his generation were all about.

Lucy: I guess. That's depressing.

James: I'm not saying that's what I think. But that's what Crane thought. Barring being adrift at sea or clobbered by an avalanche, I think people pretty much determine their fates. I think people choose their lives.

Lucy: I don't know. I think sometimes things happen to people that are beyond their control. Things that they don't want to happen.

James: I know what you're saying. Sometimes random shit happens, but for the most part, people are where they are in life because they chose to be there.

Lucy: That's not quite what I meant. It's late, James.

James: Yeah, but I think I'm going to write what I said about the sea. And I'm going to include your idea about things happening to people beyond their control. Is that okay?

Lucy: Sure. What you said about the story sounds good. It's thoughtful. You should write that down.

James: Shit. I should've been taking notes while we talked.

Lucy: Just write it down now. I'll let you go. Okay?

James: Yeah. Thanks, Lucy. I like talking to you. Hey, you can call me anytime.

Lucy: Okay. But I probably won't. Bye.

March 27, 5:45 p.m.
James: Lucy, you never told me how camping went. Did you really go camping in March? That's insane. I mean, I don't think that you're insane. Or your family. Don't take it that way. I usually go camping in June, July, or August. But it's always real buggy. I end up wearing a thick coat of Deet. I guess you don't have that problem when you camp in March. Do you sleep in yurts? Or snow caves? Just checking in with you.

March 28, 5:51 p.m.
James: Lucy, I feel a little bad about my message yes-

terday. I don't think that you're insane. I just wanted to reiterate that. Because we don't know each other. And tone can be misunderstood. You seem like a nice person. Who is totally sane. Okay. I think I need to stop talking.

March 28, 7:45 p.m.

Lucy: James, you certainly have a way with words. And tone. I actually had to look up the word "yurt" in a dictionary. No, I never went camping. Snow caves hold no appeal for me. As for sleeping in a yurt, no, I've never camped in a circular, domed, portable tent used by the nomadic Mongols of central Asia. A yurt. And you think *I'm* insane? My family and I are headed to Yellowstone in May. I'm the sort of girl who plans ahead.

March 28, 8:28 p.m.

James: Lucy, you just called. Where did you go? You're funny. Thanks for calling me. I'll be up late. You should call me back.

March 31, 3:32 p.m.

James: I got an A on my paper. I'm not calling to brag. Okay, I am calling to brag a little. But I wanted to tell you thanks. And if you're ever stuck, you should call me. Even if you're stuck in a car. Not stuck inside a car. I mean you should call me if you get a car stuck in something. Like mud. Or snow. Or a lake. Actually, if your car gets stuck in a lake, you should try to get out on your own right away and also dial 911. Why do my messages to you always sound weird?

March 31, 5:35 p.m.
Lucy: You must think I'm a lousy driver. Mud? Snow? A lake? I am an excellent driver. If I wanted, I bet I could be a long-haul trucker. A refrigerator rig and everything. Seriously. If I wanted. And the reason your messages sound weird is because they are weird.

March 31, 5:37 p.m.
James: Where did you go? You just called me. And what the hell is a refrigerator rig? Do you come from a family of truckers? Not that there's anything wrong with that. Just wondering.

March 31, 5:41 p.m.
Lucy: I think I'm in a dead zone. I'm on a walk. And where are you? *You* just called *me*. A refrigerator rig is pretty self-explanatory. It's a refrigerated semitruck. It's how perishable products get hauled across our great nation. No, I don't come from a family of truckers.

No one in my family even owns a trucker hat. In fact, no one in my family owns a car that has more than four cylinders.

March 31, 5:44 p.m.

James: You *just* called me. How can you be in a dead zone? Where are you walking? The Swiss Alps? You are the only girl I've ever met who has said the word "cylinder." It makes me wonder what other automotive verbiage you've got stuffed inside of you. Hey, when you get this, call me back.

March 31, 9:23 p.m.

James: You never called me back. Is this a sign of things to come? Lucy, Lucy, Lucy. Have you forgotten how to use your phone?

April 1, 6:45 a.m.

James: What are you doing right now?

Lucy: I'm getting ready for school.

James: Me too.

Lucy: Then why are you calling me?

James: Because it's the first day of April.

Lucy: Uh-huh.

James: And somebody might try to play a trick on you. You know, April Fools' Day.

Lucy: Are you going to play a trick on me?

James: No. I'm warning you.

Lucy: Do you know something you're not telling me?

James: No. How do you mean?

Lucy: James Rusher, you are a random person.

James: I know. So what are you going to wear to school today?

Lucy: Are you seriously asking me that question?

James: Yeah.

Lucy: Probably jeans and some sort of shirt.

Lucy: You're the reason girls thrust their fingers down their throats!

James: Calm down. If you can't touch your toes, that's no problem. Toe touches are overrated. There's a kid in my PE class whose kneecaps are too close together and he can't bend over very far at all. It's not about his fitness level. It's about his kneecaps.

Lucy: My kneecaps are normal and I can touch my toes just fine. I don't have any trouble bending over.

James: I didn't mean it that way.

Lucy: Some part of your man/boy brain totally meant it that way.

James: I hope you have a good day at school today, Lucy.

Lucy: I'm not fat.

James: I never said you were. And for the record, I'm not fat either. I play basketball.

Lucy: I'm on the track team. And, for the record, I've got above-average endurance, strength, and flexibility.

James: Above-average strength? I hope we never end up in a fight. Hey, it sounds like you've got pretty decent kneecaps, too.

Lucy: You're weird.

James: I'm also late. I've got to go. I was sort of hoping you would call and play an April Fools' Day joke on me.

Lucy: That's not my style. Are you disappointed?

James: A little.

Lucy: So you're telling me that you like a tease.

James: Maybe.

Lucy: Good to know, James.

April 1, 5:45 p.m.
James: Somebody played a joke on me today. Her

name is Beth Howie. We used to date in eighth grade. That's not really part of the joke, but I wanted you to understand that there's some history here. It was lunch. She told me there was an injured rabbit in a bush. She always really liked rabbits, and I thought maybe I could help it out. So I put on my coat and went outside and started looking at this bush. Well, there wasn't an injured rabbit in there. There was a remote control car covered with brown fur. Anyway, I'm staring at the bush and then Clay Wormser makes the fur car race out at me. So I jump back, and the fur car zooms into the street and gets hit by a truck. I swear to god. It got nailed by a semi and smashed into a million fur-covered bits. And Clay is screaming, "My car! My car!" And Beth covers her eyes with her hands and almost starts to cry. And I say, "Was that a refrigerator rig?" And Clay says, "No, it was my frigging car." And I say, "I know that. I meant the truck. It looked like a refrigerator rig." So he squints his eyes and walks into the road and starts gathering the clobbered pieces of his car, and he says, "How do you know anything about trucks?" And I say, "A friend of mine who lives in Montpelier has thought about becoming a long-haul trucker." Anyway, I thought I should call and tell you that story. Hey, do you ever talk about *me* with your friends?

April 1, 6:05 p.m.
Lucy: Technically, I live in East Montpelier. And you dated a girl whose last name is Howie?

April 1, 6:10 p.m.
James: I sure did.

April 4, 7:35 p.m.
Lucy: I'm stuck.

James: Oh my god! In your car? In a lake? I said to dial 911.

Lucy: I'm being serious here.

James: Me too. How high is the water? Wait. Maybe you're not stuck in a lake. Are you trapped in a yurt?

Lucy: Ha-ha-ha. It's an essay.

James: Why are high school students always being forced to write essays?

Lucy: I thought you liked reading.

James: Can't I digest a book without being compelled to

write an essay? Can't the education system in this country trust me to do that?

Lucy: I feel like you're joking. But you're using your serious voice.

James: Of course I'm being serious.

Lucy: You're acting like you're the one who's been saddled with the assignment. It's my essay.

James: What teenager uses the word "saddled"?

Lucy: I do. And teenage equestrians.

James: My point is that writing essays isn't a natural activity. After school, you never write essays in the real world.

Lucy: When we're in college, we'll be writing a lot more essays.

James: College isn't the real world.

Lucy: What if you become a professor? Then it would be the real world.

James: You sure do like to argue.

Lucy: You're the one who picks the fights.

James: Stop. Stop. Stop.

Lucy: Fine. Fine. Fine. But you started it.

James: Lucy, what color is your hair?

Lucy: Why? Are you going to accuse me of being a red-head? Do you live your life based on stereotypes?

James: I have brown hair. It's sort of long and curls over my ears.

Lucy: You have curly hair? Like a guy with a perm?

James: Just the ends curl. Mostly just the hair above my ears. Girls try to flick it all the time.

Lucy: What kind of girls? And what do they flick it with? Pens? Their fingers? Why are you telling me this?

James: Cute girls. They flick it with pens, pencils—

eraser end as well as graphite tip—fingers, Popsicle sticks, french fries. I get teased by cute girls. All. The. Time.

Lucy: Nobody should put french fries near another person's ears. That's a disturbing image.

James: It's not like they have ketchup on them.

Lucy: It doesn't matter. Aren't they hot?

James: The french-fry flicking only happened once. In the school cafeteria. It was a lukewarm spud.

Lucy: Moving on. I'm calling to get help with my essay, James.

James: I know. But what color is your hair?

Lucy: Maybe I don't have hair.

James: So you're a baldy. . . .

Lucy: I was kidding. That was a joke.

James: I bet you have brown hair. I bet it's straight. How long is your straight brown hair?

Lucy: I have to write a position paper. My government teacher wants me to explore two sides of an issue.

James: Why are you working on an essay on Friday night?

Lucy: It's due on Wednesday.

James: Oh god. You're a bigger overachiever than I realized.

Lucy: I wouldn't say that. It's not like I'm panting to get in to Harvard.

James: You applied to Harvard?

Lucy: No. I enjoy learning at my own pace.

James: So where did you apply?

Lucy: I don't feel like talking about college. It increases my stress level.

James: And increased stress levels lead to hair loss.

Lucy: My head-hair volume is fine.

James: You say that like I should be concerned about leg-hair volume.

Lucy: James Rusher, I am not a hairy person. Hey, stop laughing at me.

James: Okay. Okay. Do you want to know where I applied to college?

Lucy: THINKING ABOUT COLLEGE INCREASES MY STRESS LEVEL!

James: So we're not going to talk about it?

Lucy: Let's put that on the list of banned topics.

James: First you refuse to text with me. Now you're banning topics. That's very totalitarian of you.

Lucy: I never said I was perfect.

James: Okay. So what's your issue? I mean, with your essay.

Lucy: You seem to like guessing games.

James: Abortion?

Lucy: No way.

James: Euthanasia?

Lucy: Please.

James: The death penalty?

Lucy: Not even close.

James: Clubbing baby harp seals?

Lucy: The drinking age.

James: Oh.

Lucy: I think it should be eighteen.

James: You do?

Lucy: What do you think?

James: I'm probably not the best person to ask.

Lucy: But I helped you out with your paper about that open boat, and I'd never even read the story.

James: I just turned eighteen. I don't drink.

Lucy: That's partly because it's not legal, right?

James: I don't think drinking is all that important.

Lucy: This is great. It's like you're an anomaly. Because basically most guys your age not only feel they should be able to drink, but they're already drinking.

James: Yeah, it's not my thing.

Lucy: Perfect. I'll tell you my side of the issue. Then you tell me your side of the issue. Then we'll have two sides. Essay done.

James: What do you mean, "we"? *You* will have two sides. I don't need a side. I'm getting ready to take a bath.

Lucy: You take baths? You're an eighteen-year-old guy and you take baths? You're a bigger anomaly than I realized.

James: They're not bubble baths. They're just your basic bath. I like to soak my muscles. I worked out really hard today. What are you saying? Guys can't take baths now?

Lucy: I didn't think I was saying *that*. Hey, you sound upset.

James: Well, my plans are to dunk myself this evening.

Lucy: Dunk yourself? That's a weird euphemism for taking a bath.

James: This is more than a bath. I'm dunking my whole self. My body and my soul.

Lucy: Are you playing with me or are you being serious? I can't tell if you're really upset.

James: I'm not *really* upset.

Lucy: Great. Let's get to why you don't drink.

James: I don't want to.

Lucy: Why? Did you have a bad experience with it? How many times have you been drunk?

James: I've never been drunk. I think it's disgusting.

Lucy: Drinking or being drunk?

James: Both.

Lucy: Oh.

James: How is this helping you with your issue paper?

Lucy: This part isn't. I was just curious.

James: Let me help you and then I've got to go.

Lucy: You don't have to help me.

James: I think the drinking age should either stay at twenty-one or be raised higher.

Lucy: Really? How high?

James: Twenty-five.

Lucy: Holy shit.

James: That's when important parts of the brain are fully developed. Fully.

Lucy: You don't drink because you're worried about your brain development?

James: I'm answering your question.

Lucy: Do you have the science to back this up?

James: Of course there's science to back this up. I'm not pulling it out of my butt.

Lucy: Gross way to put that.

James: I'm tired, Lucy. Can't you just Google this stuff?

Lucy: That's not how I write my papers.

James: I meant for the science stuff.

Lucy: Oh.

James: I've had a long day.

Lucy: All that working out?

James: Me and Jairo had a fight.

Lucy: A bad one?

James: Yeah.

Lucy: But guys are great at moving beyond drama. It's some sort of genetic male-bond thingy.

James: There you go with your stereotypes again.

Lucy: Stereotypes are based on truth.

James: Whatever.

Lucy: I'm sorry about your fight.

James: Me too.

Lucy: Thanks for your help.

James: You're being generous. It wasn't all that useful.

Lucy: It was sort of useful. It made me realize that I need to think harder about the other side of my issue.

James: I like that. Calling me makes a girl want to think harder about her issues.

Lucy: Okay. Now I can tell that you're really upset. So what did you fight with Jairo about? Can I ask?

James: Guy stuff.

Lucy: I have no idea what that means.

James: Our fight was about a girl.

Lucy: Oh.

James: It was about a girl I used to date.

Lucy: Beth Howie?

James: No. Somebody recent.

Lucy: This sounds serious.

James: Her name is Nan.

Lucy: Is that short for Nancy?

James: No. It's just Nan.

Lucy: I've never met a Nan before. Are you *sure* it's not short for something?

James: Don't make fun of her name, Lucy. I really like her.

Lucy: I wasn't making fun of her name.

James: Yes you were. Just like you made fun of Beth Howie's last name.

Lucy: You're being hypersensitive.

James: Jairo is taking her to our senior dance. Spring Bash.

Lucy: That sucks.

James: That's an understatement.

Lucy: Would you say this is typical or atypical behavior for Jairo?

James: What are you getting at?

Lucy: Well, he recently suffered a head injury. Remember?

James: Are you talking about the tree limb?

Lucy: Yes. How would you describe the impact with his head: medium, hard, or extrahard?

James: Are you being serious?

Lucy: Of course I am. Sometimes people who suffer head injuries need another good knock to return to their senses.

James: That's not the problem. I guess they've liked each other for a while.

Lucy: I'm sorry.

James: I guess these things happen.

Lucy: I don't know if that's true. My best friend CeCe would never date one of my exes. Ever.

James: Your best friend is named CeCe and you made fun of the name Nan?

Lucy: CeCe is way more common than Nan.

James: No. It's not.

Lucy: Doesn't matter. Jairo and Nan won't last. You can't build a relationship on that kind of rocky foundation.

James: How do you know whether or not their foundation is rocky?

Lucy: I'm guessing.

James: Thanks for trying to cheer me up. It's just a dance.

Lucy: When is it?

James: Two weeks. The eighteenth.

Lucy: Take a really hot girl as your date. Show them that you don't care.

James: But I do care.

Lucy: That's so sweet of you. You've got a soft heart.

James: Wait. You just accused me of stereotyping girls based on hair color. But *you're* the one who has way too many stereotypes about *guys*. All guys have hearts. Okay. We've also got a lot of hormones. But we still have hearts.

Lucy: Maybe.

James: Ask your brother. I'm sure he'll back me up on this.

Lucy: I don't have a brother.

James: That explains a lot.

Lucy: Please. That doesn't explain anything.

James: What's your sibling situation?

Lucy: It's just me.

James: Are you an only child?

Lucy: I just told you that it's just me. What's your family situation?

James: I have a brother. His name is Bo.

Lucy: Older or younger?

James: Older.

Lucy: How old?

James: He's twenty-one.

Lucy: Is he hot?

James: Are you the type of girl who's always looking for the next best thing?

Lucy: Absolutely.

James: I don't know if Bo is hot or not.

Lucy: How many girlfriends has he had?

James: A lot.

Lucy: Then he's probably hot.

James: My bath is getting cold. I've got to go.

Lucy: I didn't realize you'd filled the tub.

James: I filled it right before you called. But I didn't want to be naked while I talked to you.

Lucy: That was thoughtful.

James: Call me and tell me how your paper turns out.

Lucy: I will.

James: I bet you get at least a C.

Lucy: Thanks for your show of confidence.

James: And I take back what I said about you being totalitarian.

Lucy: It's about time. That term doesn't really suit me.

James: I know. You like flirting too much.

Lucy: Totalitarians aren't flirts?

James: Historically speaking, no.

April 7, 6:42 a.m.
Lucy: What are you doing?

James: Getting ready for school.

Lucy: Me too.

James: Are you calling because you want to know what I'm wearing?

Lucy: No, James. I'm calling because I woke up thinking about Nan and Jairo and it made me feel bad. And it also made me want to call you.

James: Thanks. I hadn't started thinking about those two yet.

Lucy: Now I feel terrible for calling.

James: As well you should.

Lucy: But I was calling to tell you that it's going to be okay. High school is like a battleground, and this kind of drama crap happens, you know. And we move through it and go off and have great lives anyway. Become presidents. Actors. Train conductors. Professors.

James: I guess. But train conductors?

Lucy: Due to our crumbling highway system, I foresee a lot more trains in our country's future.

James: I never thought of my teen years as a battleground period.

Lucy: That's exactly what it is. Pure combat. During our teen years, things happen and we're basically put through emotional torture. Really, childhood in general is part of this too. These years test our mettle. They shape us, and then we go off toughened by our experiences. We go into the world better people. We're deepened by our traumas.

James: I didn't really think of Nan and Jairo as a trauma. I think of a brain aneurysm or falling off a tall building as a trauma.

Lucy: Trust me. Your best friend dating your ex-girlfriend is a trauma.

James: Well, thanks for calling to cheer me up. I'm going to go shoot myself in the head now.

Lucy: Don't even joke about that.

James: I know, I know. That wasn't funny. I don't have a good feel for humor at the crack of dawn.

Lucy: James, I want you to have a good day, despite those weasels.

James: I'll do my best, Lucy. Hey, I don't know your last name.

Lucy: Why do you want to know my last name all of a sudden?

James: What do you mean, "all of a sudden"?

Lucy: There's no hidden meaning in that statement.

James: Well, we're friends. I'm only asking for your last name. Why do you sound weird and defensive?

Lucy: Do you call all of your friends weird and defensive?

James: What? Are you on the lam, Lucy? Should I go to my post office and check out the FBI most-wanted list?

Lucy: It's Villaire. Lucy Villaire.

James: That's nice. Now I see why you made fun of the surname Howie.

Lucy: I shouldn't have done that.

James: We're in high school. I can't think of a more appropriate time to ridicule our peers' names.

Lucy: You were wrong. You *are* funny at the crack of dawn.

James: I'm hit and miss.

Lucy: Call me tonight.

James: I'll try, Lucy Villaire. I'll try.

Lucy: Hey, I'm wearing a skirt to school.

James: A short one?

Lucy: Short enough to show my kneecaps.

James: Nice.

April 7, 10:55 a.m.

James: Just wanted to see how that short skirt was working out. You know, you need to make sure CeCe walks behind you when going up staircases. And stick to the center of the stairs, or else you leave yourself vulnerable to peeking from below.

April 7, 11:06 a.m.

Lucy: You know a lot about how to look up a girl's skirt. No worries. I'm wearing black opaque tights. By the way, wardrobe composition is not my favorite subject. Next time we talk, I want to hear all about your favorite classes. Recent classes. Not what you liked about kindergarten or anything. I've never really gotten inside a guy's head before.

April 7, 2:55 p.m.

James: Never gotten inside a guy's head before? Lucy, you make me feel like a test subject. Like an experimental rat.

April 7, 3:10 p.m.

Lucy: I can't be responsible for your feelings, James. A very wise talk-show host once said, "Nobody can make you feel anything about yourself that you don't want to feel. You've got to give your permission." And I believe that. Also, where did you go? You just called. Okay, I'm driving home. And I always turn off my phone when I drive. Because I'm into safety. Big-time. Please don't mock me. I realize that sounded weird.

April 9, 5:38 p.m.

James: So you want to hear about my most recent favorite classes?

Lucy: I do.

James: I'm a studious type of person, so that's an easy question. My freshman year I loved a class I took called Narrative Patterns. We read *A Day No Pigs Would Die* and *The Miracle Worker*.

Lucy: Isn't *The Miracle Worker* about Helen Keller?

James: Yeah.

Lucy: You like Helen Keller?

James: I don't have a poster of her on my wall or anything, but I like her story. I like reading about people who overcome obstacles.

Lucy: Like men who get trapped inside coal mines and have to dig their way out?

James: I've never heard of anybody digging their own way out of a mine collapse. They're always rescued by outside digging. That's different. I like the stories best where people save themselves.

Lucy: I've heard about people digging their way out of avalanches. Did you hear about that guy who was out hiking and he got his arm trapped underneath a boulder, and he had to cut it off with his own pocketknife and stagger for miles to safety?

James: No.

Lucy: It was a pretty good story. And it got turned into a movie. He lived.

James: What about his arm?

Lucy: I told you. He cut it off with a pocketknife.

James: Do you want to hear more about my classes or what?

Lucy: Sure.

James: Right now I'm taking a class called the Broader World of Ideas II. We're reading a lot of *National Geographic* magazines. Next week we'll dig in to *Othello*.

Lucy: It sounds like you really like English.

James: I do. But my favorite class doesn't have anything to do with English.

Lucy: Is your favorite class Spanish?

James: No. My favorite class is Clay as an Art Form.

Lucy: Are you being serious?

James: Absolutely.

Lucy: So what are you making in there?

James: Well, a lot of my immature peers are creating art pieces that clearly have sexual origins.

Lucy: Lots of phallic pieces?

James: Oh no. My clay-sculpting peers are equal-opportunity offenders. Both male and female genitalia are being examined.

Lucy: Are they abstract pieces?

James: I wouldn't say that.

Lucy: What would you say?

James: They are what they are. And some are pretty ambitious.

Lucy: Your class sounds horny.

James: That's a good assessment.

Lucy: But what are *you* making?

James: The teacher encourages you to make utilitarian pieces as well as explore sculptural work.

Lucy: So I ask you again. What are *you* making?

James: In January I was all about making the perfect mug.

Lucy: I thought you didn't drink coffee.

James: Mugs can be used for all sorts of things. Tea, soup, ice cream. But after my mug stage, I kept with my utilitarian impulse and pursued plate making.

Lucy: How big were your plates?

James: They were plate-size.

Lucy: I see.

James: After my plate period, I moved on to sculpture. I'm currently making pieces intended for wall hanging. They reflect my interest in fly-fishing, dogs, and pie eating.

Lucy: Fly-fishing, dogs, and pie eating?

James: I fly-fish with my Grandma Rusher. She lives in Michigan. I suck at it, but she's pretty good. We go every summer. And I like dogs. All dogs. They're loyal. Pies make me happy. Even bad pies.

Lucy: I've never met anybody who could sum up their artistic influences using the words "dogs," "pies," and "fly-fishing." And does your grandpa fish too, or is it your grandma who wears the waders in that relationship?

James: Well, my grandpa did fish. But he died.

Lucy: I'm so sorry.

James: It's okay, Lucy. It happened a long time ago. He was killed in a hunting accident.

Lucy: He got shot? Guns are so dangerous.

James: No. That's not what happened. Don't turn this into a debate about that sort of stuff. He fell down a cliff. I don't want to talk about it. These things happen. It's like what you said a few phone calls ago about things happening to people beyond their control. It happened. It shouldn't have. I wish it wouldn't have. But it did. Let's get back to clay.

Lucy: Right. Your plate-making period. What do these art pieces look like?

James: Sort of like plates. But bumpier.

Lucy: You're so funny.

James: That wasn't a joke.

Lucy: It doesn't matter. Okay. I feel like I'm finally getting to know the inner James Rusher.

James: That makes me feel exposed.

Lucy: Calm down. So what was your favorite class last semester? And I want your answer to be told in the form of a story.

James: Okay. Once upon a time, last semester, I took a course called International Foods. I did this because I liked the idea of eating at school, and also learning in a room that had ovens. They were electric ovens, so that was a tad disappointing. I like flames. Anyway, while taking this course, I fell madly in love with a girl named Valley. Valley didn't seem to notice me too much. But I sure noticed Valley. She had long dark hair and she sat in front of me. Each class, I had an urge to reach out and touch her hair. When she leaned forward, her hair rose up her back. And when she sat up straight, it draped longer down her chair. It was like watching a water line climb and fall. I learned a lot that semester. Because International Foods wasn't a class just about food. We also studied food issues. Diabetes. Veganism. Hunger. Finally, things were winding to a close. Of course, it being a food class, the semester culminated with a buffet. I brought churros. They were good. My mother helped me. I'd never worked with that much hot grease before. Anyway, from across the room, I watched Valley bite into my churro, and then her face twisted into this awful expression and she spit it into her napkin. I saw her mouth ask the question "Who made these?" Well, Lucy, I liked Valley a lot, but I am also a guy who's equipped with a fair amount of culinary pride. I knew my churros were excellent. If she didn't like them, it said a lot more about her palate than it did about my churros or flash-frying skills. I saw her ask her friend again, "Who made these?" So I waved. Then she pointed to some puff pastries that involved spinach and strong cheese. I believe her dish represented Algiers. She thought her food item was superior to my churros. I watched her throw her napkin away and roll her eyes. She shook her head and flicked her hair over her shoulder and laughed.

Lucy: How rude.

James: Well, that's Valley. She has a mean streak.

Lucy: Why would you want to fall in love with somebody like that?

James: It just happened.

Lucy: I don't think it was love, James. I think you might have a hair fetish.

James: Maybe.

Lucy: How do you feel about Valley now?

James: I don't feel any way about her. I hardly see her.

Lucy: Well, then that definitely wasn't love.

James: You say that like you've been in love before.

Lucy: I was in almost-love. Once.

James: What was his name?

Lucy: Why?

James: Because I want to know his name.

Lucy: I'd prefer to give him an alias.

James: Why? Do I know him? Does he go to Burlington?

Lucy: No. He goes to Montpelier. He plays basketball.

James: I bet I know him!

Lucy: Exactly.

James: You should tell me his name right now.

Lucy: When it's anonymous, it's fun to talk about this stuff. But the idea that you might know these people freaks me out.

James: Vermont is a small state. If you want anonymous phone conversations, you should call some high school kid in Texas.

Lucy: Don't be like that. I'll tell you about this another time.

James: So you can ask me any question you want, but I can only ask you questions you feel like answering?

Lucy: I think I might be more private than you.

James: Thanks a lot.

Lucy: I didn't mean that in a bad way. I think we're just different.

James: Well, you're wrong. I'm plenty private.

Lucy: This isn't a contest.

James: It's getting late. I've got homework.

Lucy: Don't get snippy.

James: This isn't snippy. This is politely getting off the phone.

Lucy: Will you call me tomorrow?

James: Will you tell me who you were in almost-love with?

Lucy: I don't know.

James: Then I might not call.

Lucy: That's very passive-aggressive of you.

James: Will we talk about college?

Lucy: What do you mean?

James: Where we've applied.

Lucy: That could give me hives.

James: Antihistamines cure hives.

Lucy: Nothing *cures* hives. All drugs do is alleviate symptoms associated with hives.

James: You sound like a commercial. You need to lighten up.

Lucy: Okay. If you call tomorrow, I don't know if I'll tell you who I was in almost-love with, but I'll tell you a good story either way.

James: Promise?

Lucy: Yes. I promise.

James: I'll call you tomorrow, then.

Lucy: Call me late.

James: Why? What have you got going on?

Lucy: Nothing. I like talking to you late is all.

James: I'll call around eleven.

Lucy: This feels like a date.

James: When it comes to dating, you have low expectations. Financially speaking.

Lucy: So you're calling me cheap?

James: I guess I am.

Lucy: Wow. We really are strangers.

April 11, 6:38 a.m.

James: I know I was supposed to call you yesterday. I know that I didn't. I know you're getting ready for school, and you're not answering your phone because you think I'm a jerk. But I'm not. I can explain. I'll call you after school. By the way, you never told me how you did on your issue paper. I fear that means your grade might have been B range.

April 11, 3:27 p.m.

James: I'm not a complete jerk.

Lucy: I never thought you were a *complete* jerk.

James: First things first. How did you do on that issue paper?

Lucy: I got an A.

James: Why didn't you mention that earlier?

Lucy: I don't like to brag.

James: Okay. Good. Now let me explain why I didn't call you.

Lucy: It's not a big deal. But here's my stand on people who flake. If you're not sure that you can call me, then say that. If you want to leave it open, then say that. If you tell me that you're going to call me at a certain time, then you should call me at that time. Otherwise, I worry.

James: So you were worried about me?

Lucy: I like it when people call when they say they're going to call.

James: But we're not talking about people. We're talking about me.

Lucy: Yes. I was worried.

James: I like that.

Lucy: That's very selfish of you.

James: I didn't call because something bad happened.

Lucy: Were you in an accident? Are you okay?

James: There wasn't an accident. And my injuries aren't physical in nature.

Lucy: What happened to you?

James: I saw something.

Lucy: Something horrible?

James: Yes.

Lucy: Was there blood involved?

James: No.

Lucy: Can you just get to what happened?

James: It was lunch. I was walking to my locker. I had a Clif Bar in there and I wanted it. As I turned the corner, I saw them. Jairo and Nan. They were standing at Nan's locker. Kissing. Not a peck. But a deep, *let me investigate the cavern of your mouth and try to attach my tongue to your uvula* kiss. I stood and watched. Jairo kept running his hands through her hair. I heard moans. *Moans.* I felt sick, Lucy. I mean, vomit sick or passing-out sick or losing-your-shit-and-punching-someone-in-the-face sick.

Lucy: That is sick. Sounds like you really needed that Clif Bar.

James: This isn't funny, Lucy. I think they're in love.

Lucy: Don't jump to conclusions. You don't know that. They were getting it on in a hallway. And, personally, I think it's embarrassing to moan in public. Releasing those sounds in hallways lacks a certain amount of decorum. I mean, deep moaning can really travel. The janitor or principal could have heard her. Maybe even people using a nearby bathroom.

James: If she were kissing me like that, I'd release deep moans too. Wherever I happened to be. I wouldn't care who heard.

Lucy: Don't get graphic. So what did you do?

James: I thought about yelling. I thought about punching somebody in the face. But I turned around and left.

Lucy: Where did you go?

James: Lake Champlain.

Lucy: You left school?

James: I needed to think.

Lucy: You shouldn't cut class. It's a bad pattern.

James: I did it once.

Lucy: Well, if you do it again, it's a pattern. So how long did you stay at the lake?

James: Until sunset.

Lucy: Wasn't it freezing?

James: I was wearing a coat.

Lucy: Didn't your ears get cold?

James: My hair sort of covers my ears.

Lucy: How long is your hair? Do you have vicious sideburns or something?

James: Has anybody ever told you that you're not a very empathetic person?

Lucy: I'm trying to cheer you up by distracting you from your pain.

James: It's not working. It feels like you're mocking me.

Lucy: Sorry.

James: I thought Jairo was my best friend.

Lucy: Have you tried to talk to him about it?

James: Sort of. When all this started, we had a brief discussion. He said, "I think I like Nan." I said, "What are you talking about?" He said, "I want to take her to the Spring Bash." I said, "Don't be an asshole." He said, "I've felt this way about her for a while. I mean, you can't control who you like." I said, "Eat shit." He said, "Stop acting like this." I said, "Stop trying to date my girlfriend." He said, "You're not going out anymore." I said, "Jairo, you're an asshole." Then he walked off.

Lucy: That exchange doesn't exactly sound like it resolved anything.

James: God, Lucy. Imagine how this feels. What would you do if you stumbled across CeCe kissing your ex?

Lucy: I can't imagine CeCe kissing Leslie.

James: Leslie? Are you telling me that you date girls?

Lucy: No. Why would you think that?

James: The name Leslie.

Lucy: He was an exchange student from Wales.

James: An exchange student from Wales named Leslie was your last boyfriend? Is that why you didn't want to tell me his name? I don't remember a kid from Wales who played basketball.

Lucy: Leslie was my second-to-last boyfriend. But let's not talk about me. Let's get back to Jairo and Nan and you.

James: There is no "me" in the Jairo-and-Nan equation.

Lucy: You should find Beth Howie and kiss her right in front of them.

James: Why would I want to kiss Beth Howie?

Lucy: To spite them.

James: That doesn't make any sense. I broke up with Beth Howie in eighth grade.

Lucy: All I'm saying is that by kissing somebody else in front of them, you'll show them that you don't care.

James: But I do care. And I want them to care too.

Lucy: Nan is a jerk. You shouldn't like Nan anymore.

James: It takes me longer than an instant to get over somebody.

Lucy: Sometimes you're so mature it's scary.

James: Maturity scares you?

Lucy: In guys? Yes. Loads.

James: Lucy, I'm trying to have a serious conversation with you.

Lucy: I don't know what to say to make you feel better.

James: Just listen.

Lucy: Okay.

James: Seeing Nan and Jairo kiss made it more real. I can't go to the dance and see them all over each other. I might have a heart attack. It hurts that bad. Literally. The thought of those two together gives me chest pains.

Lucy: What about your date? What will she do? You can't stand her up.

James: I haven't asked anyone yet.

Lucy: Oh.

James: There is a minor complication.

Lucy: What?

James: I'm nominated to hold court. All the starters on the basketball team are.

Lucy: I don't know what that means.

James: Sort of like homecoming king, except it's not homecoming. I guess in the back of my mind, even though we were broken up, I figured I'd ask Nan.

Lucy: Forget Nan. James, you totally have to go. This could be the sort of thing you miss and then spend the rest of your life regretting. What if you win? Do you get a crown?

James: I don't know if I get a crown. But I can't go. I can't.

Lucy: You have to. Take a hot girl.

James: That's not going to solve anything.

Lucy: That's my best advice.

James: Are you sure you don't have any other advice?

Lucy: I'm pretty sure.

James: Well, what are you doing next week?

Lucy: What do you mean?

James: Lucy, would you want to go to the dance?

Lucy: You're asking me to be your date?

James: I think I'm being pretty clear.

Lucy: For your Spring Bash?

James: I know it's short notice. Do you even have a dress? Am I giving you enough time?

Lucy: Um, I have a dress. But are you sure? I mean, it could be awkward.

James: What do you mean? I bet it will be really fun.

Lucy: But what if it's weird? What if we don't like each other once we meet? What if we ruin *it*?

James: *It?*

Lucy: You know, our phone friendship.

James: Phone friendship . . .

Lucy: Don't sound annoyed. It's just, you've had time to think about asking me out, but I'm being caught off guard.

James: Okay. Never mind.

Lucy: Don't say that! Sure, um, I'd like to go.

James: Right. Of course. With your phone friend.

Lucy: We are friends. There's nothing wrong with using that word.

James: I don't ask my *friends* out on dates.

Lucy: If you'd given me more warning, I would have had a better reaction.

James: Do you always need warning time before being asked on a date? Or just with phone friends?

Lucy: James, you're not understanding me. What if, what if the person you think I am isn't the person I really am and then you end up being disappointed?

James: What are you talking about? Are you crazily different in person?

Lucy: No, not crazily.

James: Well, do you not want to meet me? Why have we spent so much time getting to know each other if you never wanted to meet me?

Lucy: You're springing this on me. I'm allowed to feel nervous.

James: Springing it? Okay. Let's stop thinking solely about Lucy and start thinking about James. I just asked you to go to a dance with me and you answered by saying "um, sure" in about the most uncertain-sounding voice ever. What about me and my nerves?

Lucy: Well, let's think about Lucy for a tiny bit longer. Imagine how it feels to know I wasn't even your first choice. You made that clear by leading with your tragic Nan story.

James: Fine. If you don't want to go with me, you should just tell me.

Lucy: I'm not saying that. I'm saying it could be weird. You might not like me.

James: You've already said that. You know what? Fine. Whatever. Clearly this was a mistake.

Lucy: Don't say that. Don't hang up. Okay. Okay. You're right. This will be fun. I'm being weird and insecure.

James: And annoying.

Lucy: Hey. That's mean. I'm trying to be super honest with you about how I'm feeling.

James: Super honest? Lucy, I like you, as more than a friend. That's why I asked you to the dance.

Lucy: Wow.

James: *Wow?* That's all you've got to say in response to what I just said?

Lucy: Wow. And, also, um, I'm not used to dealing with super honest guys.

James: I don't want to hear about other guys right now.

Lucy: Stop being angry at me. It makes me feel terrible.

James: So you really want to go with me?

Lucy: I thought I already said I did.

James: You did it in a weird, circular, Lucy way. I want to be sure that you really want to go with me.

Lucy: Point taken. Yes. Let's go. Yes. I am saying yes.

James: Good answer. Cool. Let's get down to logistics. So where do you live?

Lucy: Um. Okay. You want my address?

James: Jesus, Lucy. Are you seriously not going to give me your address?

Lucy: Calm down. That's not what I'm saying. The thing is, my address won't help you. I live in the country and it's complicated. You'll need directions, because none of the houses out here have numbers on them. And our mailbox is part of a row. So if you're coming from the north into East Montpelier, and then travel east on Township Road, I'm the fourth house on the left. It's on top of a hill.

James: If you were willing to text me this information, it would be easier.

Lucy: I'm not willing.

James: Okay. I think I got it. Fourth house on Township Road. Top of the hill.

Lucy: You can always call me if you get lost. And if you pass a giant barn with the words "Cream Dog" on it, you've gone too far.

James: What does "Cream Dog" mean?

Lucy: Probably something sexual. It's graffiti. Okay. Moving on. Logistics. Should we talk about what we're going to wear?

James: I'd sort of like to talk more about what "Cream Dog" could mean.

Lucy: Just think of the smuttiest thing ever, make it even smuttier, and you're probably close. *Moving on.* Do you want to hear about my dress?

James: Sure. Is it short?

Lucy: Stop using the tone of voice like you're still thinking about "Cream Dog." My dress is normal-length blue.

James: I have blue eyes.

Lucy: Okay. My eyes are brown.

James: This would probably be a good time to e-mail each other photos so we can see what we look like.

Lucy: I don't want to do that, James. I'm not a piece of meat.

James: I didn't want you to send me a naked picture.

Lucy: I can't believe it. I say the words "Cream Dog" and you turn into a totally different and horny person.

James: I said *not* naked.

Lucy: I'll go to the dance with you, but I'm not going to send you a photo so you can approve of my looks. That's lame.

James: Fine. I get it. So let's talk more logistics. The dance is a week from tonight.

Lucy: I know. You've already told me that.

James: I want to take you out for a nice dinner. So what do you like?

Lucy: Um, Chinese food.

James: That's easy. We'll go to Single Pebble.

Lucy: Okay. You'll have to meet my parents.

James: Are they freaky?

Lucy: They're parents.

James: Lucy Villaire, you've totally cheered me up.

Lucy: I'm glad to hear that. But when we meet, I don't want you to call me Lucy Villaire.

James: Do you go by a nickname?

Lucy: No. Lucy Villaire sounds so formal. Just call me Lucy.

James: But I'll call your parents Mrs. and Mr. Villaire, right?

Lucy: Again, that's very formal. We're a casual group. Go ahead and call them Cherry and Wolf.

James: Your parents' names are Cherry and Wolf?

Lucy: My mother's birth name is Eileen. But everybody calls her Cherry. My father's birth name is Wolf and everybody calls him Wolf.

James: Do people howl at him?

Lucy: James, do not howl at my father.

James: Okay. I won't. My parents' names are Dot and Dan.

Lucy: I'm meeting your parents? Are they, like, dance chaperones?

James: No. I was just telling you their names. Why? Do you want to meet my parents?

Lucy: Not really.

James: That's cool. It's always nice to save something for later.

Lucy: I guess.

James: Okay. This has been a long talk. I think I'm going to go for a jog.

Lucy: Seriously? It's late. Do you wear reflectors?

James: I have a vest that has reflective tape on it.

Lucy: Good.

James: Maybe we could go jogging sometime.

Lucy: How do you know that I jog?

James: You told me that you're on the track team.

Lucy: Oh yeah. Wow. You must take notes when we talk.

James: You say things that stick. Like "James, do not howl at my father."

Lucy: I'm glad you're in a better mood.

James: Love sucks, Lucy. Nan sucks. Jairo sucks.

Lucy: Love doesn't suck. That's just an awful situation.

James: Do you think it's true, what Jairo said? You can't control who you like?

Lucy: No. Nothing is that simple. You can't betray your friends.

James: That's exactly how I feel. Like they betrayed me.

Lucy: It'll get better for you. And after their relationship falls apart, they'll both feel like crap.

James: Why are you so sure their relationship will tank?

Lucy: It's sort of inevitable. We're young. We're teenagers. These are our early relationships. These aren't the people we're going to marry.

James: My parents met in high school.

Lucy: But it's really uncommon. It's more common for someone to meet their husband in college.

James: So you're telling me that I've got to wait until I'm in college before I meet my husband?

Lucy: That's exactly what I'm saying. Not that I'm counting, but that's the second time you've joked about being gay.

James: I'm comfortable with my sexuality.

Lucy: Good to know.

James: We're going to have a lot of fun. I'll call you tomorrow to talk more about it.

Lucy: You don't have to call me every day.

James: I know. If I thought I had to call you every day, then I wouldn't want to call you.

Lucy: You're such a guy.

James: Lucy Villaire, you don't know the half of it.

April 12, 2:31 p.m.
James: You sure spend a lot of time away from your cell phone. How can we continue to have meaningful conver-

sations when you don't pick up? Call me back. I've fallen into the Jairo/Nan despair pit.

April 12, 3:08 p.m.

Lucy: You need to climb out of the Jairo/Nan despair pit right away. Or, as Leslie liked to say in his small Welsh voice, straight away. You'll be okay. You're the one with the good heart and solid mind. I bet they burn through this relationship before June. If they don't, I'll eat my hat.

April 12, 4:49 p.m.

James: Nobody says "I'll eat my hat" except for my grandmother and characters in books. And why are you calling me up and talking about other guys? It's poor form, Lucy. Especially now that we have an upcoming date.

April 12, 5:24 p.m.

Lucy: I can't believe you answered your phone.

James: When I'm available, I always answer my phone.

Lucy: So your grandmother is an expert fly-fisherwoman and she says, "I'll eat my hat"?

James: Yep.

Lucy: She sounds interesting.

James: My grandmother is a bold lady.

Lucy: Bold?

James: She doesn't worry about what people think.

Lucy: Tell me a story.

James: All right, Lucy Villaire. I'll tell you a story, but then I've got to go.

Lucy: Where?

James: My friend Bensen and I are going to raise a little hell.

Lucy: I've never heard of Bensen, and you don't strike me as a hell-raiser.

James: I've been friends with Bensen since sixth grade. We both did a report on Peru. We made a topographical map together. Hey, are you yawning?

Lucy: Let's just get to your grandma story.

James: Once upon a time, when my grandma was a teenager, she stole a car. Now, this wasn't your average case of grand theft auto. She wanted to go somewhere. California. So at sixteen, she took my great-grandparents' Chevy truck.

Lucy: What year was this? America had Chevy trucks?

James: It's not polite to interrupt a story. The year was nineteen forty-something. Yes, America had Chevy trucks back then. So my grandma woke up one morning and realized that she'd never seen the ocean. So she stole the car and started driving west.

Lucy: Why didn't she head east? The Atlantic Ocean is much closer than the Pacific.

James: Interrupt me again and I end the story.

Lucy: Sorry.

James: She drove and she drove. She picked up several hitchhikers. In retrospect, it's remarkable that she wasn't robbed, cut up into pieces, and left in a ditch somewhere. But she wasn't. She drove all the way to Detroit. But when she got there, something felt wrong. As she sped toward Chicago, she felt guiltier and guiltier. She never made it past Michigan. She turned around. She cried all the way home. The end.

Lucy: Your story about your International Foods class was a lot more interesting. It had twists and stuff.

James: Here's the thing. My grandma fell in absolute love with Michigan. As soon as she turned eighteen, she moved there. She worked at a bakery and made pasties.

Lucy: What's a pastie?

James: A pastry pie filled with meat. Anyway, she met my grandpa at the bakery.

Lucy: And he liked her pasties?

James: They fell in love and got married. They lived in Michigan and took up fly-fishing.

Lucy: What did they do for jobs?

James: They ran their own bakery.

Lucy: Making pasties?

James: Pasties are a big deal in Michigan. In the Upper Peninsula they even have roadside stands.

Lucy: They serve them cold?

James: No. They heat them at the roadside stands.

Lucy: Like with propane stoves? That's dangerous. A sleepy driver or a driver on a cell phone or a crappy driver could drift off the road and hit the pastie stand and blow it up.

James: Are you being serious? How can I effectively tell my story if you're going to jump in every three seconds with bizarre anxiety issues?

Lucy: My anxiety issues aren't bizarre.

James: They are, Lucy. I was telling you a good story.

Lucy: It was okay.

James: It was about my family.

Lucy: I know.

James: It's like you're trying to miss with me. Like you want to have a fight.

Lucy: That's not true.

James: Can't we just have a normal conversation?

Lucy: We are.

James: Are you having your period?

Lucy: You did not just ask me that!

James: It's fine if you are.

Lucy: Only a jackass would say that to a girl.

James: Calm down. I didn't mean it that way. I didn't mean to make you mad.

Lucy: Yeah, because there's, like, thirty-two ways to take that question that aren't offensive.

James: I take it back.

Lucy: If we were in kindergarten, I might accept that.

James: Come on.

Lucy: CeCe is calling. I've got to go.

James: You're hanging up on me?

Lucy: It's CeCe. We're going out tonight.

James: Okay. Are you going to call me back?

Lucy: I don't know.

James: Fine.

April 12, 5:58 p.m.
   Lucy: I feel bad about our fight. CeCe and I are headed to a party in Calais. If you can call me back in the next hour, I'll be around.

April 12, 6:45 p.m.
   James: I feel bad too. I didn't mean to say that thing

about your period. I guess that was a jackass comment. Okay. You must be driving to Calais, and, for safety's sake, have turned off your phone. I'll call you tomorrow. Don't party too hard. Seriously.

April 13, 9:12 a.m.
  James: Good morning, Lucy Villaire.

  Lucy: Shh, James, why are you talking so loud?

  James: This isn't loud.

  Lucy: Softer. My head is pounding.

  James: Are you sick?

  Lucy: No. Not sick.

  James: Then what is it?

  Lucy: Ugh. I think I need some water.

  James: Do you have a hangover?

  Lucy: Maybe a little one.

James: Are you sure you're okay?

Lucy: Don't worry. I might need some Alka-Seltzer, but I'll be fine.

James: It must have been quite a party.

Lucy: Relax.

James: I am relaxed. I'm not hungover.

Lucy: It's part of life. It's not like I robbed a bank.

James: It's not part of my life.

Lucy: Softer, James. Please.

James: Why do you want to do this to yourself?

Lucy: Are you worried about my unformed brain?

James: This is a joke to you.

Lucy: Shh. Don't yell.

James: I'm talking like a normal person.

Lucy: Why are you mad at me?

James: I'm not.

Lucy: Yes you are. I can tell by the tone in your voice.

James: I'll call you when you feel better.

Lucy: I feel okay, just don't yell.

James: This isn't the best time to talk.

Lucy: Stop acting like I did something wrong. CeCe and I went to a party. I had some White Russians. I probably had one too many. It's not that big of a deal.

James: Fine.

Lucy: James, this isn't fair.

James: I can feel however I want to feel.

Lucy: But you can't treat me like crap.

James: I'm not.

Lucy: You are.

James: If you want to go out and get drunk because you think it's cool, that's your call. But I don't want you drinking when you're with me.

Lucy: You mean when we talk on the phone?

James: I'm talking about the Spring Bash.

Lucy: God, it's not like I plan on bringing my own flask.

James: You just keep joking about it.

Lucy: What's wrong with you?

James: Nothing.

Lucy: Maybe we should talk later.

James: Fine.

Lucy: Whatever.

James: Bye.

April 13, 8:54 p.m.
Lucy: Hey, James, I don't know why you were so mad at me. It's not like I go out drinking every weekend. And even if I did, you still shouldn't treat me that way. You were mean. And we're supposed to be friends. Don't do that anymore, okay? I already have a dad. His name is Wolf, remember? Talking to you used to be so much fun. What happened?

April 14, 5:52 a.m.
James: It's not fair of you to tell me that I'm acting like your dad.

Lucy: I'm not really up yet.

James: School starts in an hour and a half.

Lucy: Um, that's right. That means I sleep for another half hour.

James: I didn't realize that. Sorry.

Lucy: I don't want to fight with you. Let's not talk about drinking anymore. It's sort of like abortion or the death penalty. We have really different opinions and fighting isn't going to change anything.

James: I agree.

Lucy: All right. Well, have a good day at school.

James: This weekend will still be fun. I promise.

Lucy: You better not act like a freak again.

James: I didn't act like a freak.

Lucy: You're right. That's just the drowsiness talking.

James: You're a grumpy morning person.

Lucy: That's true.

James: Go and learn something useful today.

Lucy: I will. And James, if something happens with Jairo and Nan and you want to talk, call me. Seriously. I know that must really suck.

James: There you go reminding me about those two again. I hadn't started thinking about them yet.

Lucy: Just doing my job.

April 14, 6:46 p.m.
Lucy: I think I know why we're fighting.

James: Really? Lay it on me.

Lucy: Fear.

James: Fear?

Lucy: We're afraid of meeting each other.

James: You're afraid of meeting me?

Lucy: We're both afraid of meeting each other. Because we're total strangers.

James: Um. We're friends. I mean, I sort of feel like we've known each other for a long time now.

Lucy: Exactly. We might *feel* that way when we talk on

the phone, but in reality, you're as much of an enigma to me as I am to you.

James: Did you study Freud in your psychology class today?

Lucy: How do you know I'm taking a psychology class?

James: Lucky guess.

Lucy: Well, I think it's okay that we're afraid.

James: Okay.

Lucy: Because fear is natural. It's part of being human.

James: Uh-huh.

Lucy: Maybe we should meet in a controlled setting.

James: You don't want me to come to your house?

Lucy: Maybe we should meet in a public area first.

James: Are you afraid that I'm a criminal or something? Let's not forget, you're the one who called *me*.

Lucy: I know, I know. I just think it's important to figure out why we've been fighting so much.

James: Listen, let's not overanalyze this. We haven't been fighting that much. There was the spat about you jumping into my story about my grandmother and so I asked you about your period. And then there was the time I woke you up during your hangover. No two people get along perfectly all the time.

Lucy: I agree.

James: I think it's cool that we can call each other and talk about almost anything. It works for me. I don't think we should go digging for issues.

Lucy: So you're not afraid to meet me?

James: No. Why? Should I be? Are you a biter?

Lucy: Are you this big of a goof in person?

James: I'd say I'm worse in person.

Lucy: I've told my parents about our date.

James: Do they think it's weird that we met on the phone?

Lucy: I didn't tell them that part. I don't want to worry them.

James: So what did you tell them? Did you lie?

Lucy: I don't *like* to lie. I told them I was going to Burlington High's Spring Bash with a member of their basketball team. That was enough. Why? Do you talk about me with *your* parents?

James: No. I don't talk about girls with them. I mean, they met Nan and stuff.

Lucy: Did they like her?

James: Yeah. A lot.

Lucy: What did they say when she broke up with you? Did they still like her?

James: She didn't break up with me.

Lucy: What do you mean? I thought she dumped you.

James: No. That's not what happened.

Lucy: So you broke up with Nan?

James: Yeah.

Lucy: But you really like her.

James: Sometimes that's not enough.

Lucy: What happened?

James: We were different in some important ways.

Lucy: What ways?

James: I don't want to get into it.

Lucy: Wait. Did you love her?

James: Ugh. Maybe. I think so. I guess it was maybe-love.

Lucy: Is this the kind of instant, wimpy love you had for Valley in your International Foods class, or are we talking real love?

James: Well, I think we're talking real love.

Lucy: And you broke up with her?

James: Yes.

Lucy: That doesn't make any sense. Do you think if you told her that you maybe-love her that she would stop seeing Jairo and date you again?

James: I've thought about that.

Lucy: I can't believe that you're maybe still in love with Nan and you're not doing anything about it. I mean, you've started liking me.

James: God, Lucy. You make it sound like you want me to hang up with you right now and call Nan and profess my undying maybe-love for her.

Lucy: That's not what I want at all.

James: Nan and I are over. It had to happen. End of story.

Lucy: Are you afraid of commitment?

James: No.

Lucy: Did she do something that made you break up with her?

James: Lucy, I don't want to talk about this.

Lucy: Did she?

James: Yes.

Lucy: Does it involve Jairo?

James: No.

Lucy: My god! Did she date another one of your friends too?

James: No. That's not what happened. I don't want to talk about it.

Lucy: But I want to know.

James: Lucy, can you respect the fact that at the moment I have no desire to tell you what happened between Nan and me?

Lucy: But it sounds like she broke your heart.

James: She didn't mean to. It was complicated.

Lucy: Okay. You sound upset. I won't ask you any more questions about it.

James: It's hard for me to talk about.

Lucy: Okay.

James: It involves Bo.

Lucy: Holy shit! She dated your brother?

James: No, no, no. Lucy, I don't want to talk about it. You don't understand. My brother. Bo. He's sick.

Lucy: He has cancer? He's dying of cancer? Does Nan have cancer too? Are they both dying?

James: Lucy, you're giving me a headache. Nobody has cancer. Nan isn't sick. Nan is normal. Bo is the one who's sick. He has a problem. A drinking problem. I mean, I think he's an alcoholic. He's in rehab. I don't want to talk about it.

Lucy: Wow. Okay. I'm sorry.

James: There's nothing to be sorry about.

Lucy: This makes sense.

James: What makes sense?

Lucy: Why you got so upset when I was hungover.

James: Lucy, has anybody ever told you that you're lousy at dropping the subject and moving on?

Lucy: Yes. Many people have told me that.

James: Why don't we change gears? Why don't you tell me a story about something?

Lucy: What?

James: Your favorite class.

Lucy: I'm not a good storyteller.

James: Well, with a gripping introduction like that, I'm all ears.

Lucy: I'll do my best. I don't really have a *favorite* class.

James: Fine. Any class. I want to learn something new about you.

Lucy: Okay. Once upon a time, I took a class called Self Discovery. Hey, are you laughing?

James: Yeah. Self Discovery is one of those phrases that can have a double meaning. You know. A dirty one.

Lucy: James Rusher, I did not take a class in masturbation.

James: You are the funniest girl I've ever encountered.

Lucy: We haven't really encountered each other yet.

James: But we will. Okay. Go on. Self Discovery.

Lucy: Anyway, once upon a time, in Self Discovery, the teacher, Mrs. Scheel, asked us to sit on the floor and take off our socks and shoes. I did. Luckily, I was sporting some cute, non-odorous socks. This was not true for all of my peers. This was a risky and stinky assignment. Anyway, so there we were, on the floor, barefoot and feeling vulnerable.

James: Being barefoot makes you feel vulnerable? Have you stepped on a lot of glass in your life?

Lucy: No, James. I don't have glass-shard issues. Being in front of a big group of people with everybody's toe-jam stink wafting through the air makes me feel exposed and vulnerable. And no, I don't have hideous, weird-looking, or hammer-toed feet. I could sense that was your next question. Moving on. So Mrs. Scheel asks us to get out a pencil and some paper. She tells us, "I want you to use your feet to write your name."

James: You're joking.

Lucy: No. This is exactly what happened. I stuck my pencil between my big toe and my second toe of my right foot. I made an 'L' and then a 'U' and then I heard the girl next to me scream.

James: What was she screaming at?

Lucy: Me! Turns out, I was the only person who was able to write with my feet. The point of the lesson was to show that we're designed to function in certain ways. Something about respecting our basic anatomy and physiology. I looked like a total freak.

James: I doubt you looked like a freak. A monkey, maybe.

Lucy: I do not have long monkey toes, James.

James: Well, they're long enough to hold a pencil.

Lucy: It was a short pencil. And my toes are strong, not long. There's a difference. Stop laughing.

James: That was a great story.

Lucy: You're making me feel like a baboon.

James: Lucy, you're no baboon.

Lucy: Since we've never met, that statement doesn't exactly reassure me. It's not based on fact.

James: Then send me a picture.

Lucy: No.

James: Come on.

Lucy: No.

James: I'll send you one of me.

Lucy: Don't.

James: What's wrong with pictures?

Lucy: I like things the way they are.

James: We'll meet this Friday.

Lucy: That's how I want it. We meet. No idea what we look like. I'm in my blue dress. You're wearing a blue shirt. It will be like a movie.

James: It's not going to be like a movie. It's going to be like two people meeting for the first time.

Lucy: That's like a movie.

James: What do you think I look like?

Lucy: I don't want to play this game.

James: But you do let people take pictures of you, right? Like baby pictures, you've got those, right?

Lucy: Are you trying to get to the bottom of my neurosis?

James: Absolutely. Preferably, I'd like to uncover the bulk of them before I land on your front porch.

Lucy: Thanks for *assuming* that I've got a bulk of them, and I don't really have a porch.

James: That wasn't an assumption. It was a deduction. And how can you not have a front porch? You do live in a house, right?

Lucy: I'm not a freak of nature. Of course I live in a house. Where else would I live?

James: I don't know. Maybe a hotel. Or a Winnebago. Or a yurt.

Lucy: Nobody in Vermont lives in a hotel. Only road-tripping senior citizens live in Winnebagos. And we've already covered the yurt issue. Wow. Eleven phone calls and I've discovered two of your obsessions.

James: We've had way more than eleven phone calls.

Lucy: I don't count messages. I only count phone calls.

James: I like that you're counting. Are you using hash marks?

Lucy: Yep.

James: Okay, Lucy, so what are my obsessions?

Lucy: Yurts. And women's hair.

James: Actually, yurts don't do much for me. But I do enjoy watching a good head of hair.

Lucy: Yeah. I used to think it was just a fixation. But now I'm sure that it's a fetish.

James: You've got long brown hair. I know it.

Lucy: I've never confirmed that.

James: It's my sixth sense. I can divine hair color over the phone.

Lucy: You're so weird.

James: How is it that you can always cheer me up?

Lucy: I don't *always* cheer you up.

James: You did tonight.

Lucy: Good.

James: I'll call you tomorrow.

Lucy: I like that.

James: I like you.

Lucy: You don't even know me.

James: Sure I do. Monkey feet.

April 15, 2:24 a.m.
    Lucy: I can't sleep.

James: Lucy?

Lucy: Yes. It's me. And I can't sleep.

James: Calling people who are deep in their own sleep seems like a lousy strategy for battling insomnia.

Lucy: I don't have insomnia.

James: It's two twenty-four in the morning, Lucy.

Lucy: I know. I've been staring at my clock since eleven twenty-nine.

James: Is something wrong? Did you have a nightmare or something?

Lucy: Yes.

James: Are you okay?

Lucy: No.

James: Do you want to talk?

Lucy: Yes.

James: You're not saying anything.

Lucy: You don't want to talk about what I want to talk about.

James: How do you know?

Lucy: It's about Bo.

James: I doubt you had a dream about my brother.

Lucy: No, I didn't.

James: You're right. I don't want to talk about it.

Lucy: I *need* to talk about this.

James: Lucy, I'm only half-awake.

Lucy: Please, James.

James: No.

Lucy: I wouldn't call you in the middle of the night if it weren't important. If I didn't think you could help me.

James: Uh, geez. Here comes the guilt trip.

Lucy: Come on, James. I want to tell you about my nightmare.

James: Lucy—

Lucy: Sometimes I dream that I have a sister. And tonight I had that dream. And I want you to know that you're lucky that you have a brother. I felt like I needed to call and tell you that.

James: You have no idea what you're talking about. It's late. Let's talk in the morning.

Lucy: Okay.

James: Are you crying?

Lucy: Yes.

James: Lucy, don't cry. Okay. Tell me more about your dream.

Lucy: I was on a picnic.

James: Picnics are supposed to be fun.

Lucy: It was at first. But then it stopped being fun.

James: What happened? Did it rain?

Lucy: No. Don't minimize my dream.

James: Calm down. I'm sorry. What happened?

Lucy: Um. Okay. It was my sister. She disappeared. I

was all by myself. And it was really cold outside. I mean, I was freezing.

James: You're making your dream sound really terrible, but maybe you can look at it differently. Find a bright side. You don't have a sister, but I'm sure being an only child has its advantages. You've liked it, right?

Lucy: I'm not talking about being an only child. I'm talking about my dream. When I woke up, my teeth were chattering. I was all alone. My sister was just gone. She wasn't anywhere. It made me feel so panicked and miserable.

James: I know. But you don't have a sister.

Lucy: I'm talking about my dream! You're not listening.

James: Calm down. I am listening. Sometimes dreams can feel real. Like maybe a second life is happening while you sleep. I'm just trying to remind you that it's not real.

Lucy: I've had this dream before. A lot. And it kills me.

James: Well, try to look at it a different way. At least you get to know what it feels like to have a sister. Even if it's in your second life. Even if she eventually disappears. God, Lucy, you're really crying. Calm down.

Lucy: But I don't want her to disappear!

James: I think you're overtired. This has happened to me before. It feels like your whole world is falling apart. But it's not. You just need to get some sleep. You'll be okay.

Lucy: You're so lucky to have a brother. I bet he doesn't mean to be an alcoholic. And he's in treatment. It sounds like he's trying.

James: Lucy, I don't want you to talk about Bo anymore. Just calm down. You're okay. Focus on what you have.

Lucy: I know. I know.

James: Everything is fine. You've got a great life. It was just a lousy picnic dream.

Lucy: It feels so real.

James: Take deep breaths.

Lucy: Okay.

James: I'll call you tomorrow. I promise. We'll have a long talk after school.

Lucy: I really like that. It means a lot that I can call you like this. I mean, I've never called anybody like this before.

James: Yeah.

Lucy: Am I freaking you out by telling you these things?

James: No, Lucy. I care about you.

Lucy: I feel the same way. It's just that you're better at expressing yourself. You're lucky like that.

James: Stop crying, Lucy. We'll talk in the morning.

Lucy: Yeah. I want to finish this conversation. I'm not through talking about these things.

James: Yeah. Okay. But remember, no Bo.

Lucy: I know. I get it. I'll try not to bring him up anymore.

James: Promise?

Lucy: Yeah.

James: I want to feel like I can tell you things.

Lucy: Me too.

James: Feel better and go back to sleep.

Lucy: I'll do my best.

James: No more picnics.

Lucy: Okay. Okay. You too.

James: Oh, I wouldn't mind dreaming about a picnic. As long as there aren't any hornets, or vicious off-leash dogs, or stinging ants.

Lucy: You can't always turn everything into a joke. Some things aren't supposed to be funny.

James: Good night, Lucy. Sweet dreams.

Lucy: Night.

April 16, 6:31 a.m.
James: Are you getting ready for school?

Lucy: Yes.

James: Are you feeling better?

Lucy: Yeah, but not perfect.

James: Feeling perfect seems unrealistic.

Lucy: Well, I'm a very impractical person.

James: If I asked you what you were wearing to school today, would you call me a pervert?

Lucy: I'm not going to wear a skirt.

James: Do you think that's all I'm interested in hearing about?

Lucy: Oh, please. Have you suddenly become curious about women's fashion? Do you want me to break down my wardrobe for you?

James: Maybe.

Lucy: What do you want to know?

James: What's your favorite color to wear?

Lucy: Brown.

James: Brown?

Lucy: It looks good with baby blue. And pink. And also green. And cream. And red. And tan.

James: You're right. I don't want to hear about this. Just have a good day, okay?

Lucy: Do you want me to call you at lunch?

James: Sure.

Lucy: Am I starting to call you too much?

James: No. Don't worry about that. If it gets to be too much, I'll just stop answering my phone.

Lucy: What a jerk!

James: I was kidding.

Lucy: There was a seed of truth in what you said. I could feel it.

James: Lucy, I'm not the kind of guy who burns through girls.

Lucy: That's exactly what I'd expect a guy who burns through girls to say to me.

James: Are you trying to start another fight?

Lucy: No. I'm not like that.

James: You're totally like that.

Lucy: Not on purpose.

James: You're a very accidentally contentious person.

Lucy: I'm a nice girl.

James: I know, Lucy. You're sweet.

Lucy: Like pecan pie.

James: Ugh. I hate pecan pie.

Lucy: I thought you said you liked pie. I thought it was one of your main artistic influences.

James: Only fruit pies speak to my muse.

Lucy: Your muse?

James: My source of inspiration.

Lucy: So no cream pies?

James: Absolutely not.

Lucy: Huh. You sound like you've got a tricky palate. What's your favorite dessert?

James: My favorite dessert isn't pie.

Lucy: Figures.

James: It's cake. I love carrot cake.

Lucy: You're joking.

James: This isn't the sort of thing I'd joke about. I worship carrot cake. With extrathick cream-cheese frosting.

Lucy: James Rusher, you are a total freak. Carrot cake? What self-respecting teenager prefers carrot cake to way-better cakes? Like German chocolate cake. Or devil's food cake.

James: Thanks for calling my self-respect into question and relabeling me a freak. I hope you have a good Wednesday too.

Lucy: Thanks. And thanks for last night.

James: You don't have to thank me for that kind of stuff. I want to be there for you.

Lucy: I'm not used to being with guys who say things like that.

James: First, let's not talk about other guys. Second, I'm not just saying things. I mean that.

Lucy: Let's talk later.

James: Deal.

April 16, 10:56 a.m.
Lucy: James, you'll never guess what they're serving in the cafeteria. Well, Hawaiian pizza and green salad with Hidden Valley ranch dressing, but that's not the most interesting lunch component. They're serving carrot cake! I don't think this has ever happened in the history of Montpelier High School. Seriously. I was so shocked, I bought a piece and I wrapped it in napkins and I'm putting it in my locker and I'm going to take it home and freeze it and give it to you on Friday. Okay. Talk to you later. Carrot cake!

April 16, 11:18 a.m.

James: It's sounds like you're putting that cake through an uphill battle. And cake doesn't have any instincts of self-preservation. It's cake. So if CeCe decides that she'd like to eat it, or if you get a craving for it, either of you should feel free to tackle it.

April 16, 7:24 p.m.

Lucy: I can't believe you don't want the cake.

James: I can't believe that you can't believe that I don't want the cake.

Lucy: But it doesn't look like it's been through a war. It's held up really well. It's in my freezer right now.

James: If it lasts until Friday, I promise to eat it.

Lucy: Oh, you'll eat it.

James: I've never been threatened with carrot cake before.

Lucy: Get used to it.

James: Are you being serious?

Lucy: No.

James: I've got a pile of homework. I have to finish a report on Teddy Roosevelt.

Lucy: A big one?

James: Just five pages.

Lucy: What's your focus?

James: The Rough Riders.

Lucy: You're writing a report about Teddy Roosevelt and condoms?

James: Are you trying to be funny?

Lucy: I don't think so.

James: I'm writing a report about Teddy Roosevelt and his military role in the Rough Riders.

Lucy: Do you need any help?

James: What do you know about the first United States Volunteer Cavalry regiment during the Spanish-American War?

Lucy: Very little.

James: Then I think I'll go it alone.

Lucy: Call if you get stuck.

James: Don't worry, I will.

Lucy: I'm not worried.

James: Good.

Lucy: Does this mean we're not going to have our long talk?

James: Do you want to have our long talk?

Lucy: I'm feeling okay tonight.

James: Then is it okay if we save it for later?

Lucy: Like the carrot cake . . .

James: Exactly. Just stick your emotions in the freezer and thaw them out for me later.

Lucy: Are you telling me that I have emotional problems?

James: Not problems. I'm just pointing out the obvious. Lucy Villaire, you've got emotions.

Lucy: Yeah.

James: Call me later if you want.

Lucy: Enjoy writing about the Rough Riders.

James: It won't be that bad. I sort of like Teddy Roosevelt.

Lucy: As much as Helen Keller?

James: You need to lay off Helen Keller.

Lucy: I didn't realize I was on her.

April 16, 9:37 p.m.
Lucy: I just found out that I don't have shoes.

James: How is that possible?

Lucy: I mean for the dance.

James: Just wear anything.

Lucy: I can't do that. It's a dance, James.

James: I know it's a dance. I invited you to it.

Lucy: I think I'm going to buy a pair of those pumps that you dye to match the dress.

James: Okay.

Lucy: You don't have issues with those?

James: Pumps?

Lucy: Dyed-to-match shoes.

James: No. I don't have issues with dyed-to-match shoes.

Lucy: That's a relief.

James: Just tell me the dye formula and I'll match my pants to your shoes.

Lucy: No respectable store would dye a pair of pants for you.

James: Then I'll do it myself in my bathtub.

Lucy: You won't.

James: Don't dare me, Lucy. I always rise to dares.

Lucy: I'll let you get back to your report.

James: Did you know that the Rough Riders were a completely volunteer fighting force? They were a bunch of cowboys and Ivy League athletes and glee club singers and Texas Rangers and miners and Indians.

Lucy: But they were trained, right?

James: Yeah, they were trained in Texas and then they were transported to Cuba. And in the confusion surrounding their transport from Tampa, half the members of the Rough Riders were left behind, along with all their horses. The Rough Riders charged up Kettle Hill and San Juan Hill on foot.

Lucy: We fought against Spain in a war? In Cuba?

James: Yes. And the Rough Riders had a really high casualty rate. The highest of all the regiments in Cuba.

Lucy: Well, they were miners and glee club singers.

James: I don't really like reading about war, but I think history is pretty mind-blowing. I like reading about the survivors.

Lucy: Do you like history as much as Clay as an Art Form?

James: You're jealous of my clay class, aren't you?

Lucy: Of course.

James: Maybe I'll make you something.

Lucy: I don't want anything sexual.

James: I wasn't planning on sculpting you a vagina.

Lucy: I can't believe you just said the word "vagina."

James: You just said it too.

Lucy: I think it's time to say good-bye.

James: You're very delicate when it comes to discussing anatomy.

Lucy: I know.

James: That's not a criticism. I can work with delicate.

Lucy: Good to hear.

April 17, 6:56 a.m.
James: You must be in the shower. Or maybe you've gone to get your shoes dyed. I finished my report about the Rough Riders. You know, most of the kids in my class hadn't even heard of the Rough Riders. I think that explains a lot about our country. Lucy, sometimes I think

I want to move somewhere else and live my life there, where people are more in touch with all the ways their country has struggled. Like the Czech Republic. Have you ever thought about that? Living somewhere else? Call me later if you want.

April 17, 7:10 a.m.
   Lucy: I wasn't in the shower. And I wasn't getting my shoes dyed either. I was picking CeCe up for school. She built a diorama of Robert Browning's poem "My Last Duchess." It uses a considerable amount of toothpicks, tongue depressors, cellophane, and small twigs. It also involves a triple-A battery. Hers is a very fragile diorama. I mean, it isn't the sort of thing you can take on the bus or set in the backseat while you drive yourself to school. It's the kind of project you have to hold on your lap while your best friend drives twenty miles per hour over Vermont's potentially diorama-wrecking hills. But I didn't mind, because it's an awesome diorama. Have you ever read that poem? It's about murder. It's actually told from the point of view of the murderer. Until CeCe said this, I had no idea. I thought it was a poem about a painting. I thought the speaker of the poem was the same as the person who wrote the poem. But that's not the case. Because Robert Browning apparently never killed anybody. I bet if the title

said that it was told from the point of view of the guy who murdered the duchess, a lot more people would read it. Nobody reads poems anymore. I think it's because of the lousy titles. Wow. What a long message. Talk later.

April 17, 10:42 a.m.
James: It's lunch. No carrot cake. And no diorama around to look at either. I have to be honest, Lucy. Diorama making strikes me as a fourth-grade activity. What are they teaching you at East Montpelier? Hey, I'm bored. You should call me.

April 17, 11:15 a.m.
Lucy: A guy who plays with clay and churro dough for high school credit should not judge people who build dioramas.

April 17, 3:23 p.m.
Lucy: You'll never guess what happened today.

James: Somebody blew up your school.

Lucy: That's not funny. In fact, I don't even think you're allowed to make jokes about bombs and schools anymore. Public or private.

James: Are you going to turn me in?

Lucy: Let's drop this.

James: Okay.

Lucy: The thing that happened today is diorama related.

James: CeCe dropped her diorama.

Lucy: Yes!

James: Did it break?

Lucy: Are you kidding? Of course it broke. It practically exploded.

James: Did this happen before or after it was graded?

Lucy: Before.

James: Ouch.

Lucy: It's okay. The diorama project was pass/fail. CeCe threw herself into it for personal reasons. Her mortal enemy, Ginny Loomis, had chosen the same poem for her assignment. CeCe didn't want to be second best.

James: Did everyone build a diorama? Did you build a diorama?

Lucy: Yes.

James: How come you didn't tell me about your diorama?

Lucy: I knew you'd mock it.

James: Come on. That's not fair. I might have teased you a little, but that's to be expected.

Lucy: I guess I'm just sensitive.

James: That's one word for it.

Lucy: Hey!

James: I want to hear about your diorama. No joking around. I promise.

Lucy: Okay. Mine wasn't elaborate like CeCe's.

James: Sounds like hers had structural issues anyway.

Lucy: You said no joking around.

James: I meant about *your* diorama.

Lucy: Well, I figured you meant all dioramas.

James: Sheesh. I had no idea you had such serious hang-ups regarding craft projects.

Lucy: One more insensitive comment and I'm hanging up. Don't push me, James Rusher. I'll do it. It only takes a push of the thumb.

James: Okay. Don't hang up. Keep your thumb where it is and tell me about what you built.

Lucy: Well, it had to be about a poem.

James: So what lousy title did you choose?

Lucy: I don't think that all poems have lousy titles. When I said that, I was just thinking out loud.

James: Go on.

Lucy: The subject had to be a poem written during the Victorian Era. I chose "Goblin Market" by Christina Rossetti.

James: I think I've read that. It's about two girls, right?

Lucy: Yeah, it's about these two sisters, Lizzie and Laura, who get tricked by a group of Goblin men.

James: Goblin men are always trying to trick innocent sisters with alliterative names in poems.

Lucy: Alliterative?

James: Alliteration is when consonants are repeated.

Lucy: I know what alliteration is. I've just never heard the word "alliterative." Whatever. So the Goblin men trick Laura into cutting a piece of her hair and giving it to them as payment for this magic fruit. Then she eats it and gets really sick. I mean, she starts to die. And so Lizzie has to risk her life to go and get more fruit.

James: So what did you do for a diorama?

Lucy: I used a shoe box. I put stickers all over the back wall and then tucked two small dolls in it. I also put a bunch of fake cherries in the box to represent the magic fruit.

James: What about the Goblin men?

Lucy: I cut out black shadows and stuck them on the wall with the stickers.

James: What are the dolls doing?

Lucy: They're just sitting there. On a blanket. It's not like I had to animate the diorama.

James: Did it have a lid?

Lucy: Why are you suddenly referring to my diorama in the past tense? Yes, it has a lid. I cut an eyehole out at the front of the box, so you can look in and see what's going on.

James: Isn't it dark?

Lucy: It's a little dark. But you can still see the fruit and dolls and Goblin men shadows.

James: It sounds good.

Lucy: It's fine.

James: I'm sure you'll pass. Hey, I just thought of something. I bet the reason you had your dream about losing your sister is because you built that diorama.

Lucy: I guess.

James: What do you mean, "I guess"? It's so obvious.

Lucy: I've had that dream before. When I wasn't making a diorama.

James: Well, what triggered it this time was the diorama. I'm sure.

Lucy: I don't want to talk about my nightmare. Moving on. My shoes will be ready tomorrow.

James: Wow. Good to hear, because I've been stressed out about that all day.

Lucy: Very funny. So when exactly are you picking me up?

James: I thought I'd pick you up at exactly five o'clock.

Lucy: That seems early.

James: It will take about an hour to drive back to Burlington. I think five o'clock is sort of late.

Lucy: Really? You can pick me up earlier if you want.

James: I'll pick you up at four thirty. Exactly.

Lucy: Are you the sort of person that if it starts snowing a lot, you won't drive on the freeway?

James: We're not going to get heavy snow in April.

Lucy: It *could* happen.

James: It's highly unlikely.

Lucy: Weather patterns keep getting crazier and crazier. I stand by my question. If it starts snowing a lot, are you the sort of person who won't drive on the freeway?

James: No.

Lucy: Good.

James: Why? Are you worried that I'm not going to come?

Lucy: I was just wondering if severe road conditions alter you.

James: They have to get pretty severe before I consider myself "altered."

Lucy: This is good to hear. Besides, I already checked NOAA and things look pretty clear. There might be a light snow. But apparently snow doesn't stop you. Now I don't have anything to worry about.

James: So enough time has gone by since your last psychology class that you don't think we're still afraid to meet each other?

Lucy: Yes. Time passed and I got over feeling that way.

James: Good.

Lucy: I think we'll have a great time.

James: So you're not worried that things might feel awkward?

Lucy: No.

James: You sound so sure.

Lucy: James Rusher, I think we have a genuine connection.

James: You do?

Lucy: I really do.

James: That can only be jeopardized by road conditions?

Lucy: Let's drop that. I was just curious if a snowstorm could ruin things. But it doesn't sound like that's the case. I think this all goes back to our genuine connection.

James: It's good to know you feel that way. Because I might need to lean on that while being forced to confront the Nan/Jairo connection.

Lucy: I try not to think about those two being at the same dance.

James: Oh, they'll be there.

Lucy: Let's just ignore them.

James: I don't know. I sort of think I should talk to them. I haven't talked to them since Jairo and I had our fight.

Lucy: They both sound like selfish pigs.

James: So I should never talk to either one of them ever again?

Lucy: Pretty much.

James: I think I might be more forgiving than you, Lucy.

Lucy: I don't want to meet them.

James: Couldn't you at least say hi?

Lucy: I don't want to.

James: But what if I want you to?

Lucy: They seem like really crappy people. Especially Nan.

James: You don't even know them.

Lucy: Well, I know what you've told me about them.

James: They have their good points.

Lucy: James, you've spent weeks telling me how awful they are and I believe you. Can't you talk to them when I go to the bathroom or something?

James: It's weird to me that you might hate them more than I hate them.

Lucy: Well, I guess I'm weird. I'm just saying that I've developed strong negative feelings for them, and if you want to be safe, you better keep us apart. Or I might say something or do something crazy.

James: Crazy?

Lucy: Sometimes I yell at people.

James: You cannot yell at my dance.

Lucy: If I see her and she says something shitty, I can't make any promises.

James: Oh, you're going to make me that promise right now.

Lucy: No.

James: Lucy, I can't take you to the dance if you're going to go off on my ex-girlfriend.

Lucy: Keep us apart.

James: You don't even know who she is or what she looks like and I can't really keep her from approaching me.

Lucy: I just want to have fun with you, James. And interacting with toxic people will kill that.

James: Did I call them toxic?

Lucy: No, but you used a bunch of other negative language.

James: Okay. I'm not saying that I know for sure

whether I'll talk to either one of them. But if I do, if that's what I decide to do, I want to make sure that you're not going to act psycho.

Lucy: I have never acted "psycho" before in my whole life. I'm a civilized person. I'm not going to punch anybody in the face.

James: I know that. I just think maybe we could smile and stuff.

Lucy: I like the idea of staying separated.

James: Yeah, but what if I want to ask Nan for one dance? Maybe you could dance with Jairo for one dance.

Lucy: What planet do you live on? Your ex-girlfriend is going to the prom with your best friend. And you've asked me to be your date. You've told me that you like me. You can't go off dancing with your ex-girlfriend in front of me. In this situation, it just isn't done.

James: You make my life and my judgment sound so awful when you talk about it like this.

Lucy: It's not awful. But you've got to follow some obvious rules of etiquette.

James: Yeah. You're right. I'm just trying to figure out how to handle the dance.

Lucy: Separation. Avoidance. You've got plenty of options. Also, I'm not jealous of Nan.

James: I never said that you were.

Lucy: But that's what you were starting to think, isn't it?

James: No. I was starting to think that I don't know what the hell I'm going to do when I see Jairo and Nan tomorrow night.

Lucy: You're supposed to pretend like they don't exist and dance your ass off.

James: Lucy, that seems like a game.

Lucy: It's not a game. It's a strategy for protecting your heart. And your image.

James: I don't care about my image.

Lucy: That's probably because your reputation is in good standing. But forcing a weird Nan encounter at the dance could change that.

James: I guess you're right.

Lucy: I know I'm right.

James: You're sounding really bossy tonight.

Lucy: It's only the afternoon.

James: Even that sounded bossy.

Lucy: I didn't mean to be bossy.

James: Yeah. Okay. I've got homework.

Lucy: Are you going to call me later?

James: I'm not trying to blow you off. I've really got homework. I'm working on a report about America's invasion of Grenada.

Lucy: For what class?

James: History.

Lucy: But you just finished a report on the Rough Riders for that class.

James: I've got a report due every week for the rest of the year in history.

Lucy: That's too many. Especially for somebody who is anti-essay.

James: I don't mind writing these. It's for history.

Lucy: You sound depressed.

James: I'm not. I've just got a lot on my mind.

Lucy: Is this about our date? I don't want our date to stress you out.

James: That's not it. I'm looking forward to finally meeting you. Really. And I feel so much better knowing that you won't be punching anybody in the face.

Lucy: Ha-ha. But I didn't say anything about not kicking certain people in the knee. Or the no-no spot.

James: The no-no spot? What are we, ten-year-olds? I'm glad you can have a sense of humor about this.

Lucy: I'm glad that you're glad.

James: I'll call you tomorrow. I mean, I'll *see* you tomorrow.

Lucy: Does that mean you won't call me?

James: Do you want me to call you? Does that make our meeting more like a movie or less for you?

Lucy: Um, good question. I guess less.

James: So you don't want me to call?

Lucy: Um.

James: You're nervous.

Lucy: No. Maybe. I don't know why I'm sounding like this. I'm actually really excited.

James: Okay. How about I call you after I exit in Montpelier?

Lucy: Okay. Do you need me to give you directions again?

James: I have them. Township Road. Fourth house. If I see the words "Cream Dog," I've gone too far.

Lucy: Right. So, four thirty tomorrow.

James: Exactly.

Lucy: Wow. Exactly.

April 18, 4:45 p.m.
Lucy: You're late. Are you lost? Did you hit traffic in Burlington? Hmmm. Call me. Okay?

April 18, 5:10 p.m.
Lucy: If you don't get here soon, I'm going to think that you were in some sort of horrible accident. Seriously. Where are you? I'm totally ready. I even have your boutonniere in my refrigerator. I also put the carrot cake in there to thaw out. Okay. Maybe you thought we said five o'clock. Maybe you aren't *that* late.

April 18, 5:38 p.m.

Lucy: I just tried to find your home number in the phone book. Then I called the operator. It's unlisted, James. God, maybe you don't even exist or something. Or maybe you said you were James Rusher, but you're not really James Rusher. Maybe you're some creep named Neil or Alexander or Ted. What's going on? Where are you? It's totally messed up to be this late. I'm worried. I'm angry. God! The road conditions are perfect. I've checked NOAA six times. Just get here, okay?

April 18, sent 5:43 p.m.

Lucy: Are you okay? Are you coming? I'm worried about you. You said "exactly." So now you're late and you're a liar.

April 18, 6:21 p.m.

Lucy: So we're not going to the dance. Because it will be too late now. Or maybe we could go to the dance and skip dinner. I'll call Single Pebble and cancel our reservation. I really think you've been in an accident. I'm going to start calling hospitals. So if you got cold feet or you somehow patched things up with Nan and you're just standing me up, you need to suck it up right now and not be a coward *and* a jerkface and tell me that immediately. Because after hospitals, I might start calling morgues. Seriously. I'm breaking out in hives. All over. I'm so worried. Where are you?

April 19, 1:14 a.m.
Lucy: You're either the biggest asshole on the planet Earth, or you're dead. Either way, don't ever call me again.

April 19

April 20

April 21, 8:51 p.m.
Lucy: Your phone still works. So you can't be dead. You *are* just an asshole. I can't believe it. What was the point of all this? Just to make another person feel like shit? Mission accomplished. If you ever feel tempted to call me again, don't. Burn my number.

April 22

April 23, 4:46 p.m.
James: Lucy, I am so sorry. I know you don't want to talk to me. This isn't entirely my fault. There was a family emergency. My mom picked me up from school. I forgot

my cell phone. I had to go to Canada. These aren't just lame excuses. I didn't have your phone number. But it wouldn't have mattered, because I didn't have cell phone reception in Montreal. When I was at the hospital, I tried to find your home number online. But I couldn't find a Villaire anywhere in Vermont. I thought about calling one of your friends, but I didn't know CeCe's last name. I want to fix things. I'm so sorry that I worried you. I feel awful about your hives. I didn't mean to do this. I am so sorry. I'll take you for a nice dinner at Single Pebble. I'll take you to another dance. I'll take you anywhere. I like you. I didn't mean to hurt you. Please call me.

April 24, 6:21 p.m.

James: You might think that I sent the flowers because two days ago was Earth Day and tomorrow is Arbor Day. But I sent them because I still feel bad and I want to talk to you. We're friends, Lucy. Friends should forgive each other. This was beyond my control. It's like I was one of those guys bobbing in the sea in Crane's story. My fate was out of my hands. There was nothing I could do. Come on. Call me back.

April 25, 6:34 a.m.

James: I thought maybe if I called you in the morning

you'd talk to me. Lucy, I miss talking to you. I feel bad. I wish that hadn't happened. Why don't you call me back? Think about it.

April 25, sent 12:09 p.m.
James: You should answer your phone. We'd both feel better.

April 25, 3:39 p.m.
James: Even if you aren't answering your phone, I figure that I can leave you messages about my day. I talked to Jairo today. He felt bad about my family emergency. Nan too. She found me and we talked at lunch. I don't want to tell your voice mailbox about that situation. I'd rather tell you. I'm not trying to be mysterious about it. It's just that it's personal. Anyway, it felt good to talk to Jairo. And you were right about him and Nan. Things are rocky. I don't think the foundation was all that great. Good call on your part. I don't know if me and Jairo will be great friends again or anything. And talking to Nan was a little weird. I should just forgive both of them and move on. How about this, you forgive me and I'll forgive them? Everybody wins. Especially me. That was a joke. Maybe next time I call, you'll pick up your phone. Maybe.

April 27, 2:34 p.m.

James: Lucy, this is ridiculous. I should just drive out to your house and force you to have a conversation with me. You're being way too stubborn. Answer your phone. Just talk to me.

Would it be that hard to do that? I said I was sorry. What more can I do? Tell me! Is this really how you want things to end?

April 27, 2:35 p.m.

James: You're acting like a baby! I forgot to tell you that in my last message. *Whah. Whah. Whah.*

April 27, 2:41 p.m.

James: I shouldn't have yelled at you in my last message. I'm sorry. I just want to talk to you. I want to fix this. Pick. Up. The. Phone.

April 28, 5:28 p.m.

James: This is a serious call. I have something important to tell you. It's about Bo. I've been thinking about him a lot. And I've been thinking about what you said after you had your picnic dream. The one where your second-life sister disappears. There's a good reason why I'm mad at Bo. God, Lucy, I wish I was talking to you. I want to be friends with you again and have somebody who can see my life the way I see my life. Would that be so bad? Okay. I'm going to tell you something that I never tell anyone. Before Bo went into rehab, he went to a party. It was a stupid, out-of-control party in Waterbury and when he got home, he did something. It was bad. Something nobody should ever do, no matter how sick they are. It made me hate him. Anyway, while he's been away, he's been writing me these letters. I'm pretty sure they're apologies. But I never open them. I shove them in an old ski boot in my closet. But because of you, because of you not forgiving me, I understand how much forgiveness matters. Being unforgiven is the worst. It's shit. So I'm going to start reading his letters. I don't know if I'll read them all. I got another one yesterday. That's what I'm going to be doing all night. I'd really like it if you'd call me. I didn't hurt you on purpose. I'm not an asshole. If I could change things, I would. Seriously. And Lucy, what does all this silence really accomplish? Does it make you feel better? Are you happy like this?

April 28, 10:51 p.m.
   Lucy: Hey.

   James: Finally.

Lucy: I might hang up at any time.

James: No. Don't say that. Don't hang up. Come on.

Lucy: So what happened?

James: With Bo or with my family emergency?

Lucy: I'd assumed the family emergency was about Bo.

James: No. It was my grandmother.

Lucy: Is she okay?

James: No. She's sick.

Lucy: Does she have cancer?

James: No. Why do you always think somebody I know has cancer? That's weird and pessimistic.

Lucy: Lots of people have cancer. And you keep using the word "sick." And that can mean cancer. Because some people don't like to use the word "cancer," because it's frightening.

James: Fine. No, she's sick in another way.

Lucy: Heart disease?

James: God, Lucy, I'm not trying to make you guess. If you were quiet for two seconds, I'd tell you.

Lucy: So tell me.

James: The doctors don't quite know what she has. She gets in her car to go somewhere basic, like the gas station or grocery store, but she doesn't stop driving. She leaves the city. The state. This last time she left the country.

Lucy: Did she get in a wreck?

James: No. She's a good driver. That's not the problem. The best way I can say it is she's going senile.

Lucy: That's why you were in Canada?

James: Yeah. She got in her car and didn't stop and the police found her sleeping in a parking lot near the Biodome.

Lucy: Does she have Alzheimer's disease?

James: No. It's not that. It's different. After the police found her, they took her to the hospital.

Lucy: Is she still in the hospital?

James: No. She's staying with us.

Lucy: Is her car still in Canada?

James: No. I drove it home.

Lucy: Do you have to hide her car keys?

James: Lucy, this isn't a joke. It's a dangerous situation. She goes to some messed-up place and becomes totally unreachable.

Lucy: Does she forget who you are? Because this totally sounds like Alzheimer's disease.

James: It's not that. They've done tests. They're sure.

Lucy: Doctors are wrong about things all the time. Even cancer.

James: These doctors aren't wrong. What's with you? Why can't you just let me talk about this?

Lucy: I'm sorry.

James: She can't live in Michigan anymore. She can't live by herself.

Lucy: Does she like living with you?

James: I think so. But she's asked me for my car keys about twenty times.

Lucy: Where does she want to go?

James: Everywhere. The laundromat. The hardware store. The library.

Lucy: Do you take her?

James: She doesn't need to go. She just wants to go.

Lucy: Is she bored?

James: I thought that. What happens is she gets all

dressed up. Nylons. Lipstick. Scarf. Then, she writes a note and puts it on the refrigerator. Then, she grabs her purse and asks me for the keys.

Lucy: And what do you say?

James: I tell her that the car is broken.

Lucy: You lie to her?

James: It's the easiest way to handle it.

Lucy: Doesn't it bother you, though, that you're lying to her?

James: Since I'm keeping her safe, it doesn't bother me that much.

Lucy: Oh.

James: I think lying is rotten. I'm not a natural-born liar. But in this situation, it's the best thing.

Lucy: Okay. So, what's new?

James: That's an awkward transition. Come on. What was going on with you? We don't talk for eleven days. You don't return any of my calls. You made me feel so awful. I listened to your messages. I know I made you worry and I hurt your feelings, but you wouldn't even listen to what I had to say.

Lucy: That's not true. I listened to your messages.

James: But you never picked up. And you never called me back.

Lucy: I know I should have called you back sooner.

James: Why didn't you?

Lucy: It's complicated. I'm complicated.

James: Does that mean you're not going to tell me?

Lucy: Yes.

James: You're so frustrating. Are you ready to hang up?

Lucy: No.

James: What do you want to talk about, then?

Lucy: Something that you probably don't want to talk about.

James: Bo?

Lucy: Yes.

James: Why are you so curious about my brother?

Lucy: I just am.

James: You want to hear about the letters. I knew you would. I've only read four so far. It's slowgoing.

Lucy: How many has he sent you?

James: At least twenty.

Lucy: And you never read any until now?

James: No.

Lucy: That's rotten of you.

James: Don't judge me, Lucy. That's not fair. I'm not in the best headspace right now.

Lucy: Can I ask you something before you talk about the letters?

James: Sure.

Lucy: What did Bo do?

James: What do you mean?

Lucy: You said that after he got back from a party that he did something awful before he went into rehab. What did he do?

James: It's hard for me to talk about.

Lucy: Did he hurt somebody?

James: Not in the way that you're thinking.

Lucy: How do you know what I'm thinking?

James: He didn't physically hurt anybody besides himself.

Lucy: What happened?

James: He lost control.

Lucy: What does that mean?

James: He just went crazy one night. It was the most awful thing I'd ever seen.

Lucy: What did he do?

James: I don't want to go there.

Lucy: Did he try to kill himself?

James: Lucy, stop. I've just told you some serious personal shit about my grandmother and my brother, which I never do. For the first time in your life can you respect some boundaries? God! You're so frustrating. Do you have any idea how I'm feeling? Can you be a friend to me?

Lucy: I understand what you're saying. Yes, I can be a friend.

James: Okay, but I'm tired of talking on the phone. I think we should meet.

Lucy: I think we should talk on the phone some more.

James: Really?

Lucy: Things have gotten weird. You stood me up. It made me feel fragile. And now we're making all these personal confessions and stuff. This feels different.

James: First, I had a family emergency. You can't hold that against me. Second, you haven't made any personal confessions. And you basically dragged what I said out of me.

Lucy: But you have to agree that this feels weird now.

James: No. If we talked face-to-face—

Lucy: James, I'm not ready to meet.

James: You're impossible.

Lucy: Don't say that. Take a breath. Okay. James, I need to tell you something.

James: What?

Lucy: Well, I can't tell you right now.

James: Why, do you have to go somewhere?

Lucy: No.

James: Then what is it? You need to stop being so obnoxious. It's stupid and mean to jerk me around like this.

Lucy: Stop judging me. I want to tell you something that I don't talk about with people. Ever.

James: And I'm telling you that I want to hear it. So tell me.

Lucy: Not yet. You should read more of Bo's letters. I'll call you later.

James: No. Tell me now or don't tell me. Ever.

Lucy: You don't mean that.

James: I actually think that I do.

Lucy: When I tell you what I haven't told you, it's going to make you feel really terrible.

James: Is that why you aren't telling me? Because you're trying to protect my feelings?

Lucy: Well—

James: I feel emotionally wiped. I can't keep having conversations like this with you.

Lucy: I want things to be like they were before.

James: That's impossible. Shit has happened. You can't rewind the past.

Lucy: I know.

James: Are you crying, Lucy?

Lucy: I just feel so overwhelmed.

James: I can't keep talking. I can't do this right now.

Lucy: Can we talk later?

James: I don't know if I can keep having this conversation. What's the point?

Lucy: Please don't sound so mad.

James: I'm frustrated.

Lucy: You're not the only one going through hard stuff.

James: It's not my fault if you don't know how to talk about your problems. You can't take that out on me.

Lucy: I'm trying my best.

James: I'm not the kind of person who's going to wait forever.

Lucy: Yeah. I figured.

James: Okay. We'll talk later.

Lucy: Promise?

James: You know we'll talk.

Lucy: I just wish you wouldn't sound so mad.

April 29, 7:34 p.m.
James: Hey.

Lucy: Hey.

James: Just checking to see if you'll answer when I call.

Lucy: Do you have trust issues with me now?

James: Did you have your psychology class again today, Lucy?

Lucy: Is it that obvious?

James: It is. Hey. I just want to make sure that we can move past that last call. I mean, move forward.

Lucy: You say that like you want me to do something.

James: Yeah, well. I want you to talk to me.

Lucy: James, I am talking to you. We're rebuilding. Remember. You *did* stand me up.

James: God, Lucy, that's so unfair to say considering the circumstances. I mean, I was out of the country!

Lucy: I know. I shouldn't use that against you. I shouldn't have said that.

James: What am I to you?

Lucy: You're James.

James: No. Am I a phone friend? A guy you like? How do you think of me? I mean, what are we? What if I told you that I wanted to date somebody at my school?

Lucy: I wouldn't want to hear that. You know that. I already said that I like you.

James: (Silence followed by a sigh.)

Lucy: You're not thinking about getting back together with Nan, are you?

James: No.

Lucy: Well, is there somebody else you like?

James: I just said that to see what you'd say. There isn't anybody.

Lucy: That's mean.

James: What would you do if I drove out to your house right now?

Lucy: Um, nothing. I'm at CeCe's.

James: Where does she live?

Lucy: I'm not going to tell you. I don't want you to drive out here.

James: Not only are you secretive, you're scared and confused.

Lucy: No, I'm cautious. Okay. Maybe I'm a little overly cautious.

James: No, you're confused. And just so you know, in life, overly cautious people end up missing out.

Lucy: Overly cautious people live longer.

James: Not necessarily. And those that do have boring lives. Like tortoises. They live excruciatingly long, cautious, boring lives.

Lucy: Don't compare me to a tortoise.

James: Prove me wrong. Let me come see you. Let's be normal people. Let's date.

Lucy: I'm already a normal person and I don't have to prove anything to you. I want to hang up.

James: Just a couple of minutes ago you said you liked me and now you want to hang up. You're erratic.

Lucy: When did our relationship devolve into unprovoked name calling? I'm a tortoise? I'm not exciting? Now I'm erratic?

James: You're right. We should talk later.

Lucy: Buh-bye.

April 29, 9:20 p.m.
Lucy: If I'm erratic, then you're repressed.

James: What are you talking about?

Lucy: It's true. You're very muffled when it comes to your emotions.

James: You're calling me emotionally muffled?

Lucy: Yes.

James: I don't even think that's a thing.

Lucy: Sure it is.

James: Well, I don't think it's a bad thing.

Lucy: It could be. If you're so muffled that I can't understand you.

James: You're the one who doesn't know how to talk to me about what's going on with you. You already admitted to that. So quit trying to pin stuff on me.

Lucy: Every time we talk, you seem pissed at me.

James: I'm annoyed.

Lucy: Can we have a nonangry conversation? What are you doing right now?

James: I'm finishing a report on the Philippine-American War.

Lucy: For somebody who doesn't like writing essays or reading about war, you seem rather obsessed with both activities.

James: I don't want to be the kind of American who doesn't know basic shit.

Lucy: I don't think that the Philippine-American War is basic shit. I think that's advanced.

James: Right. But it *should* be basic shit. We should know which countries our military has invaded or bombed or occupied, and why.

Lucy: We'll probably learn all that stuff in college.

James: Why wait?

Lucy: It's only a few months away.

James: Since you brought it up, I think it's time that we finally start talking about college.

Lucy: No.

James: Yes.

Lucy: It will make me itch.

James: But we've already gotten acceptance letters, right? You've been accepted.

Lucy: Maybe.

James: Just answer the question.

Lucy: Yes.

James: Where?

Lucy: Why?

James: Lucy, stop being difficult and tell me where you got accepted.

Lucy: How come you're in such a bad mood all the time?

James: You're frustrating me to the point of insanity.

Lucy: Okay. I've been accepted at UMass Amherst, University of New Hampshire, Bowdoin, and UVM.

James: I'm going to UVM. Not that you asked.

Lucy: Oh.

James: You sound so thrilled.

Lucy: No. That's cool. If I go there too, maybe we could take a class together or something.

James: Or something? I need to go.

Lucy: I just don't want to make too many plans about the future. Sometimes things change suddenly.

James: Got it. I need to get back to work.

April 30, 8:12 p.m.
Lucy: I never thanked you for the flowers.

James: Nope, you didn't.

Lucy: They were lovely. So thank you.

James: They're already dead?

Lucy: Most of them.

James: You didn't save any of them by hanging them upside down?

Lucy: How did you know that girls do that? Is that what Nan and Beth Howie did?

James: Sometimes I think that you're obsessed with my ex-girlfriends.

Lucy: Okay. I've got one word for you.

James: What?

Lucy: Greg Tandy.

James: That's two words.

Lucy: I can't believe you don't realize what I'm telling you.

James: What? What about Greg Tandy?

Lucy: He is my ex-boyfriend.

James: Really? The guy you loved?

Lucy: Calm down. It was almost-love.

James: Greg Tandy is a great forward. One of the best in the state.

Lucy: Vermont is a small state. I doubt there's all that many forwards.

James: Ouch. So I take it the breakup wasn't friendly?

Lucy: When are breakups ever all that friendly?

James: So what happened?

Lucy: Long story short: He dumped me.

James: Why? Was there somebody else in the picture?

Lucy: No. I guess it's more accurate to say that I hurt him and then he dumped me.

James: Did you kick him in his no-no spot?

Lucy: I *so* regret using that term with you.

James: I like that you did.

Lucy: James, sometimes I hurt people by not being able to give them what they want.

James: Oh.

Lucy: But I'm working on it.

James: Are you talking about sex?

Lucy: Not exactly.

James: But partly?

Lucy: Maybe. Yeah. I don't know exactly.

James: Is that new ground for you?

Lucy: James, I am not going to talk about the state of my "ground" with you.

James: You're the one who brought it up.

Lucy: I know. But I've said all that I want to say about it for now. I was calling to thank you for the flowers. That's all. I have to go.

James: I'm sorry about Greg Tandy. He was sort of a thug on the court. Lots of elbows. But he was pretty wimpy about taking hits. He overreacted to the tiniest bump. Always flopping for the foul. He was never my favorite.

Lucy: You don't have to trash Greg to cheer me up.

James: I'm just being honest.

Lucy: Me too.

James: I guess we're just a couple of honest people. Maybe that's what drew us together.

Lucy: Maybe. Can I ask you something serious? And it's not about Bo.

James: Sure.

Lucy: How is your grandma?

James: Oh, she seems to be doing fine. Sometimes I take her for drives. She likes to sing along to the radio.

Lucy: Has she driven anywhere yet?

James: No. She probably won't drive again.

Lucy: That's so sad.

James: It's for her own good.

Lucy: But when she was sixteen, she drove away to get a new life, and even though she went back to her family for a while, driving changed her whole future.

James: She's old now. She doesn't need to drive. I'll take her where she needs to go.

Lucy: But she doesn't have her freedom anymore. Don't you worry that she feels like she's living in a prison?

James: I live in a pretty nice house.

Lucy: That's not what I mean. She isn't able to do what she wants to do.

James: There's no perfect solution. I can't send her off on I-89 and hope for the best.

Lucy: I know.

James: This is a good compromise.

Lucy: Does she still ask if she can drive?

James: Yeah.

Lucy: If you're taking her for rides, she knows that the car isn't broken.

James: I tell her that her driver's license has expired.

Lucy: Is that the truth?

James: It will be in two months. I mean, it's practically the truth.

Lucy: Oh.

James: I don't normally lie. You don't need to worry about that. When my grandmother isn't slipping into a senile condition and asking for the keys to my mother's Subaru, I'm a very honest person. I promise.

Lucy: I hope she gets better.

James: I don't think people with her condition get better.

Lucy: Maybe she needs another doctor. Sometimes doctors screw up. After surgeries, sometimes they leave sponges inside of people and sew them back up. And sometimes they amputate the wrong leg.

James: You have real doctor issues.

Lucy: I'm a cautious person.

James: The doctor isn't the problem in this situation, Lucy. My grandma is sick.

Lucy: Well, I hope she *feels* better.

James: Me too.

May 1, 5:49 a.m.
James: I just thought of something and I want to talk about it with you.

Lucy: It's too early to be thinking and talking.

James: What I'm thinking is related to a dream I had. Have you ever heard the saying "I'll sleep when I'm dead"?

Lucy: You're thinking about death?

James: I just had a dream and I want to talk to you about it before I forget it. I always forget them.

Lucy: You should get a notebook and write your dreams down in it. Keep the notebook by your bed. A lot of people do this.

James: I don't have *that* many dreams.

Lucy: How would you know? Maybe you're just forgetting them.

James: Fine. I'll buy a notebook.

Lucy: You could probably just use one that you already have.

James: Okay. Fine. I'll find a notebook.

Lucy: Good. Does this mean you'll share your dreams with me?

James: You're talking too much. Can't you listen? I have to get ready for school and I feel like I'm forgetting my dream even as we speak.

Lucy: Yes. I'll listen. Go ahead. Tell me about your dream.

James: I dreamed about a slate plaque.

Lucy: Sounds like a boring night.

James: It made me think of the plaque maker.

Lucy: And?

James: Did you ever call that guy? What happened? I mean, it's the whole reason our lives ever intersected, and we just stopped talking about it.

Lucy: We moved on to better things. Hey, I'm wearing a skirt today.

James: Lucy, I don't want to hear about your skirt.

Lucy: Wow. When you dream about plaques, you become a totally different person.

James: Don't mock me this early in the morning.

Lucy: I don't consider this mocking. Now, if I start emitting monkey sounds, then you can accuse me of mockery.

James: You're all weird this morning.

Lucy: I'm getting ready for school and I'm tired.

James: Back to my dream. And the slate plaque. Lucy, did you ever call the guy?

Lucy: Yes.

James: Really? Because in my dream you called him! Wow.

Lucy: I don't think it rises to the level of "wow."

James: What happened?

Lucy: We talked.

James: Yeah. But what did you say? Did you give him a piece of your mind?

Lucy: I don't know. Maybe.

James: That doesn't make any sense. Of course you know whether or not you gave him a piece of your mind.

Lucy: I guess I mean that what I said is personal.

James: You told the plaque maker personal things?

Lucy: Yes.

James: Like the things you tell me?

Lucy: No. Um, more personal.

James: Seriously? Why did you do that?

Lucy: I needed to.

James: Are you saying this because you're tired and just being random?

Lucy: I'm not being random. I'm saying it because it's the truth.

James: Did the plaque maker want you to tell him personal things?

Lucy: Yes.

James: Well, that's creepy. Is he some sort of Svengali?

Lucy: A what?

James: A villain. Somebody who manipulates other people.

Lucy: You're not making any sense.

James: I'm not making any sense? I'm not the one pouring my heart out to a deadbeat trophy maker.

Lucy: He's just a person. You sound so angry.

James: You sound so different. Sad.

Lucy: I'm freakishly tired, James. Therefore, I lack pep.

James: No, this isn't fatigue. It's sadness. I can tell the difference.

Lucy: Are you sure you don't want to talk about my skirt instead?

James: Yeah.

Lucy: I don't want to talk about the plaque maker.

James: You know, you don't want to talk about a lot of things with me.

Lucy: Did you call me up to point out my flaws?

James: What's wrong with you this morning?

Lucy: Nothing! I wasn't ready to have a serious discussion yet. That's all.

James: Did something happen besides the plaque maker? Something with CeCe?

Lucy: No. Why would you think something happened with CeCe? That's weird.

James: She's the only person in your life who you talk about.

Lucy: The only person in your life who you talk about is Jairo.

James: And Nan.

Lucy: Right. Nan.

James: And Bo.

Lucy: *Barely.*

James: And my grandmother.

Lucy: I don't have any living grandmothers to talk about with you.

James: How come it took you so long to tell me Greg Tandy's name?

Lucy: I don't think it took me *that* long.

James: How come you never told me that you called the plaque maker?

Lucy: I thought we were trying to talk about things that mattered with each other.

James: Well, you just told me that you told the plaque maker personal things. So now I want to hear all about it.

Lucy: You're possessive.

James: I'm not possessive. You're secretive.

Lucy: Okay. Talking to the plaque maker isn't a happy story for me.

James: What did that asshole say to you?

Lucy: Calm down. He's not an asshole.

James: Did you used to date this guy or something?

Lucy: Did you recently hit your head? I think that guy is at least forty. *At least.* Why are you asking me such lame questions?

James: So what did you tell him?

Lucy: I told him a story about my plaque and reminded him that I'd already paid. Then he agreed to ship it to me.

James: Some guy who quit his company and fled to New Jersey is suddenly going to do the right thing and ship you your plaque? He's lying.

Lucy: I don't think he's lying. He apologized for his behavior.

James: And you just forgave this asshole and now everything is fine?

Lucy: Pretty much.

James: You omit tons of stuff when we talk.

Lucy: You're way too hung up on my slate plaque.

James: Until I dragged it out of you, you never told me about your diorama. Or dating Greg Tandy. Or calling the plaque maker. And it took you forever before you told me where you lived. Plus, you never talk about your parents.

Lucy: You don't talk about your parents either.

James: We're talking about *you* and *your* hang-ups.

Lucy: Everybody has hang-ups. I'm not perfect. You're not perfect!

James: When you start crying, it makes it hard to talk to you.

Lucy: You're the one who's making me cry. And I need to get ready for school.

James: Okay. Fine. We'll talk later.

Lucy: Not if it's going to be like this.

James: What do you mean? You don't want to talk anymore?

Lucy: You're accusing me of too many things and acting like a crazy person.

James: No, I'm not. I'm being normal.

Lucy: I'll be the judge of that.

May 2, 3:14 p.m.
Lucy: I never told you about the plaque maker because I didn't think you'd care. Also, there's something about my plaque I never told you, but I'm not really ready to tell you yet, okay?

May 2, 4:19 p.m.
James: Of course I care about the plaque maker. I care

about anything that you care about. And as far as with-holding a story about your plaque, that makes no sense to me. But I know how to respect boundaries. So *I* won't hound you about it. I won't even bring it up again. I'll just wait for you to tell me.

May 3, 8:48 a.m.
   Lucy: I'm calling because I want to lighten things up.

   James: It's Saturday morning. What makes you so sure that I'm awake?

   Lucy: I was so eager to achieve my goal of lightening things up that I overlooked the fact that you might not be conscious yet.

   James: I'm conscious. Lighten away.

   Lucy: I have a pet.

   James: When did you get a dog?

   Lucy: Oh. I don't have a dog. I have a way better pet than that.

James: A cat?

Lucy: No.

James: A rabbit?

Lucy: Try again.

James: Fish?

Lucy: Closer.

James: A lizard?

Lucy: Nope.

James: Turtle?

Lucy: *Nein*. That means "no" in German.

James: I know that.

Lucy: Guess again.

James: I give up, Lucy. What pet do you have?

Lucy: You gave up way too easily.

James: A ferret?

Lucy: Uh-uh.

James: A hermit crab.

Lucy: No way.

James: Is it a form of insect?

Lucy: No. Do you give up?

James: I thought I gave up at turtle.

Lucy: I have a parakeet.

James: But when I guessed fish, you told me that I was close.

Lucy: Right. Because a cat will eat a fish or a parakeet, because it's a predaceous animal. My pet is a prey animal.

James: Your logic baffles me.

Lucy: My logic works.

James: What's your parakeet's name?

Lucy: Santiago.

James: You named your parakeet after the capital of Chile?

Lucy: I'd never thought of that.

James: Okay. How long have you had Santiago?

Lucy: Six years.

James: That's a long time to withhold your parakeet ownership from me.

Lucy: I didn't withhold it. It just never came up.

James: So when we finally meet each other, will I get to see Santiago?

Lucy: I don't think so.

James: So far, I don't feel much "lightening up" going on in this phone call.

Lucy: Well, Santiago doesn't live with me anymore.

James: Did he escape?

Lucy: No. He's in a box at CeCe's. We mated Santiago with her parakeet, Paris.

James: You mated two parakeets named Santiago and Paris? What are you hoping to yield from that?

Lucy: Baby parakeets!

James: Aren't pet parakeets difficult to mate?

Lucy: Well, they have to like each other. And they need a nesting box, because apparently they need the darkness. It helps Paris's hormone level and kicks in her parenting instincts. And the cage has to be between seventy and eighty degrees Fahrenheit.

James: Naturally. So Paris is the girl?

Lucy: Yes. Paris is the girl keet and Santiago is the boy keet. And for a long time Paris wouldn't even sit on the same perch with Santiago.

James: Well, if your keets don't like each other, it sounds freakishly implausible that you're going to wind up with eggs, let alone baby parakeets.

Lucy: But we've got eggs! Paris laid them yesterday! Five!

James: Is that a normal amount?

Lucy: That's actually a very good question. Because egg laying is demanding on their bodies. And parakeets can get into a mode where they don't stop laying eggs. They lay them and lay them until they die.

James: Wow. That's a disturbing image.

Lucy: I know.

James: So five is a good number?

Lucy: It's a great number. But Paris did strain herself a

little on the last egg and CeCe had to rub olive oil around Paris's cloaca. Do you know what a cloaca is?

James: I can guess what it is.

Lucy: The eggs will hatch nidicolous. That means that they stay in the nest until they're ready to fly. They grow fast. They'll be ready to leave the nest in a few weeks.

James: Can you see the eggs?

Lucy: A little. They're in the nesting box.

James: Now that's something I'd like to get a peek at.

Lucy: Well, I'm not ready to show you my eggs.

James: I figured that would be your answer.

Lucy: I didn't mean that in a sexual way.

James: Even if I took that comment as an anatomical reference to yourself, it really wouldn't have been sexual. The thought of eggs doesn't turn me on. It's like saying the word "sperm" is sexual.

Lucy: Saying the word "sperm" is totally sexual. I mean, that's what's released during sex.

James: Lucy, I'm aware of that.

Lucy: I'm just saying.

James: This conversation has taken a turn toward the bizarre.

Lucy: I agree. When I called you, I was hoping we could return our talks to a more normal place. But this. Talking about my eggs. And your sperm. That's not the normal place.

James: I'm not talking about your eggs. Or my sperm. We're discussing Paris.

Lucy: Right.

James: So when will they hatch?

Lucy: In about eighteen days. Unless Paris tries to eat the shells off the eggs.

James: Why would Paris do that?

Lucy: She'd do it if her calcium levels were low. You know, it takes a lot to lay an egg, James.

James: I imagine it does. Are you going to record the hatchings?

Lucy: That's a great idea!

James: Do you need a camera?

Lucy: Maybe.

James: I might have something to offer you yet.

Lucy: You'd mail me your camera to borrow?

James: No. I'd bring it.

Lucy: I know I'm being lame about not meeting you sooner.

James: Finally.

Lucy: But I like this idea.

James: Do you want to meet sooner?

Lucy: I've got a crazy schedule these next couple of weeks. My parents want me to tour colleges with them.

James: Will you be up in Burlington?

Lucy: With my parents. I'm not meeting you with my parents.

James: Okay.

Lucy: I like the idea that our first encounter would be the hatching of my eggs. That's more like a movie than the first time we were supposed to meet.

James: You and our movie-worthy first meeting. You've made it way more suspenseful than it needed to be. How will I know when to come?

Lucy: It will be some time in the next eighteen days.

James: You don't want to set the camera up earlier to capture everything?

Lucy: Not really.

James: Will you call me and tell me exactly when to come?

Lucy: Absolutely.

James: Should I bring anything besides my camera?

Lucy: Like what?

James: I don't know.

Lucy: Just bring yourself.

James: I might bring something else.

Lucy: What?

James: It will be a surprise.

Lucy: Should I have a surprise for you, too?

James: I don't need a surprise.

Lucy: Well, if you insist.

James: You can get me a surprise if you want to.

Lucy: I knew you wanted a surprise.

James: Okay. We'll each bring a surprise.

Lucy: But nothing naughty.

James: What do you think I was planning to bring? Porn?

Lucy: Don't say things that make me feel lame.

James: When I say "porn," it makes you feel lame?

Lucy: You need to stop saying the word "porn" immediately.

James: Okay.

Lucy: So what are you going to do today?

James: It looks like things are warming up. I'll probably go for a run. What about you? Hey, how's track going? Are you training for anything?

Lucy: I don't want to talk about track.

James: Why?

Lucy: I just don't.

James: Why?

Lucy: Because.

James: Because why?

Lucy: I quit it.

James: You quit? When?

Lucy: March.

James: But we've been talking since March and you told me that you ran track.

Lucy: Did I say that *exactly*?

James: Yes. *Exactly*.

Lucy: Oh.

James: Why would you lie about that?

Lucy: I didn't lie.

James: You're either a member of the track team or you're not a member of the track team. Which is it?

Lucy: Well, if you put it that way, I'm not a member of the track team.

James: Then you weren't totally honest with me.

Lucy: You're right.

James: Why not?

Lucy: James, I wanted this to be a light conversation, but now we're treading into serious waters again.

James: We are? Because of track? Did you suffer some sort of injury?

Lucy: James, I sort of have *limitations*.

James: What does that mean? You had to give up track because of a physical condition?

Lucy: Oh, my limitations aren't physical.

James: I have no idea what you're trying to tell me.

Lucy: Is it that important that I tell you right now?

James: Yes.

Lucy: Okay.

James: You're not saying anything.

Lucy: I'm deciding how to phrase it.

James: Just spit it out.

Lucy: *Pth. Pth.*

James: What are you doing?

Lucy: Making spitting noises.

James: Lucy, stop kidding around and tell me why you quit track *and* why you lied to me about it.

Lucy: Okay. Okay.

James: I'm still waiting.

Lucy: James, I am an emotionally limited person.

James: So you had to quit track for emotional reasons?

Lucy: Sort of.

James: You need to do a better job explaining this.

Lucy: I can't.

James: You mean you won't.

Lucy: No. I can't. It's part of my emotional limitations. It's part of why I don't text-message people. It's part of why it took me so long to call you back.

James: You're starting to freak me out.

Lucy: Don't say that. I'm opening up to you.

James: Yeah, but in a way that confuses me.

Lucy: I think I'm done talking about this.

James: So that's it? No more explaining?

Lucy: I'll explain more later. But not now.

James: What else do you want to talk about?

Lucy: I think I'm done talking altogether.

James: Forever?

Lucy: For now.

James: Lucy, every time we talk, you get more and more puzzling.

Lucy: I'm not trying to do that.

James: Now I need to go take an aspirin.

Lucy: When you say that I cause headaches, it hurts my feelings.

James: I'm only being honest.

Lucy: And a tad mean. Making up is a process.

James: An excruciatingly long one, apparently.

May 5, 12:12 a.m.
James: You didn't call me today and I didn't call you.

Lucy: I'm aware of that.

James: Did you have a good day?

Lucy: I guess so. I'm sort of half-asleep and not all that interested in thinking too hard.

James: But I want to talk. I've been reading Bo's letters and there's things in there I want to tell you about.

Lucy: Really?

James: Yeah. It's good that I'm reading them.

Lucy: What kind of stuff do you want to tell me about?

James: I thought you wanted to go to bed.

Lucy: I'm starting to feel more awake.

James: I think he's really sorry.

Lucy: For being an alcoholic?

James: No. For what he did.

Lucy: I still don't know what he did.

James: Do you want to know?

Lucy: Only if you want to tell me.

James: I don't like talking about it.

Lucy: Then you don't have to.

James: When you don't push me, and you act like how you are now, it makes me want to tell you.

Lucy: I never meant to push. I'm just curious.

James: What Bo did is really bad.

Lucy: I know. You've already said that.

James: Like, television bad.

Lucy: You don't have to tell me.

James: But now I want to.

Lucy: Okay. I'm listening.

James: Bo got back from the party and he snapped. He'd been dating this girl, Cecil, and they'd broken up, and he saw her at the party. He got home and reached a breaking point and just snapped.

Lucy: So you were there.

James: Yeah. It was me and my mom and my dad. I've never told anybody about this.

Lucy: Do you want me to ask questions or just be quiet?

James: Just listen.

Lucy: Okay.

James: He was angry again. He always got angry when he drank. He got home and was yelling about Cecil and her friend, who wouldn't even talk to him at the party. I was in my room. My parents were downstairs watching television. And I heard my mom screaming. It wasn't even a specific word or anything. But the sound she made cut into me. Then I heard my dad yell, "Put down the gun." It was so surreal. It felt like I was listening to a movie, except the voices were all familiar. I mean, my god, it was my dad yelling that. I ran downstairs. I remember turning the corner and seeing my mother's face. I can't even describe it. It was an expression of total suffering. Like something sharp was piercing her heart. My dad had his hand out. And he said it again, "Put down the gun." I kept moving. Around the corner. That's when I saw Bo. He was crying. His face was wet from tears and snot and sweat. He had my dad's handgun. It was in his mouth. Out of instinct, I jumped toward him. I don't know what I thought I was doing. Bo stepped back and I saw his finger move. He pulled the trigger. *Click. Click. Click.* Three times. I thought his head was going to explode. I thought I was going to see his skull burst. But nothing happened. He pulled the gun out of his mouth and threw it on the floor.

Lucy: So it wasn't loaded?

James: It was. But it only had one bullet in it.

Lucy: Was he trying to kill himself?

James: I don't know what he was *trying* to do. He was wasted. He fell onto the floor. I couldn't even understand what he was saying.

Lucy: And then he went to rehab?

James: That morning.

Lucy: Did you have an intervention?

James: After something like that happens, you don't try to negotiate a rehab plan. You just take him. But I can still hear that click. And I can still smell him. It was vodka and sweat. And then vomit. Because he puked on the floor. My mother went over and sat him up. She rolled him out of his own mess. She was crying. Begging him to sit up.

But he was so blitzed. Like an enormous drunk baby. At first I hated Cecil for making him feel like this. But then I hated him. I hated him for making us go through this. Over and over.

Lucy: Yeah. It doesn't sound like it was Cecil's fault. Or her friend.

James: I get that.

Lucy: He'd done that with a gun before?

James: No, it was the first time with the gun. But he was always coming home smashed. Or getting loaded in his room. It's like he just couldn't deal with life.

Lucy: Some people are predisposed for addiction.

James: I guess. But at a certain point I think people choose their own lives. Yeah, Cecil broke up with him. Yeah, she ignored him at a party. But Bo is still responsible for what he does.

Lucy: I'm sure he doesn't want to be an alcoholic.

James: I know, I know. I'm reading his letters. I know he's sorry. He regrets what he's done. I think he's getting better.

Lucy: That's good.

James: But I don't know if I'll ever trust him again. I mean, once somebody takes you down that road. What do you do?

Lucy: I think you have to try to trust them.

James: I'm not there yet.

Lucy: I think it's okay if this takes time.

James: It's not that easy. None of this is that easy.

Lucy: I'm not saying it's easy. I'm trying to make you feel okay about stuff.

James: I wish these things didn't happen. I mean, it's like all those wars I read about. Yeah, some people survive. But I wish all that stuff never had to happen.

Lucy: I feel the same way.

James: That's why I broke up with Nan.

Lucy: Because she liked wars?

James: No, because she always drank on the weekends. Usually it was just beer. But this once, at a party, she drank vodka. And the smell . . . It made me want to throw up. And when I looked at her, I didn't just see her. I saw Bo, too. And it was too much.

Lucy: Are you telling me that Nan's an alcoholic?

James: No, Nan likes to drink. It's a social thing for her. I told her that I couldn't deal with it. She said I was too controlling and that she liked the buzz. So I broke up with her.

Lucy: Because she drank vodka one time at a party?

James: It didn't work for me to have a girlfriend who drank and who didn't understand how it affected me.

Lucy: Oh.

James: And it's not just vodka. The smell of any booze makes me physically ill.

Lucy: So you won't even drink when you're in college?

James: I don't think so. You know, not everybody drinks in college. It's not like freshman composition. It isn't a requirement.

Lucy: I know. I guess if you don't want to, then you shouldn't.

James: I can't believe I told you about this.

Lucy: Did it make you feel better?

James: Yeah. But only because Bo is doing well. If he was still stumbling around the kitchen shitfaced, I'd probably feel differently about sharing this story.

Lucy: I'm glad you told me.

James: Listen, I get the feeling there's some things you'd like to tell me, too.

Lucy: I'm not ready. I mean, we've already covered a lot of ground tonight.

James: I know. But it was all my ground.

Lucy: It might have been *your* ground, but my heart is literally racing.

James: I know. It was an awful story.

Lucy: I hate awful stories.

James: Everybody hates awful stories.

Lucy: People who read Stephen King novels don't seem to mind them.

James: Ha-ha.

Lucy: It's late.

James: Yeah. But, Lucy, whenever you're ready to talk to me, I want you to know that you can tell me anything.

Lucy: Anything?

James: Yes.

Lucy: Are you sure?

James: Positive.

Lucy: Okay. Good night, James.

May 5, 6:23 p.m.
Lucy: I've been thinking about what you said about being honest.

James: Yeah.

Lucy: You're right.

James: About what?

Lucy: I haven't been totally honest with you.

James: Okay.

Lucy: It's related to my limitations.

James: This is not the sort of phone call I expected to get from you on Cinco de Mayo, but I'm listening.

Lucy: I'm being serious.

James: So am I.

Lucy: I need to tell you something before we meet.

James: Is it about track?

Lucy: No, it's a larger issue.

James: Okay. Spit it out.

Lucy: It's not that easy.

James: Do you want me to try to guess?

Lucy: It's nothing you'd be able to guess.

James: Is it about the plaque maker?

Lucy: I'm not joking around.

James: Neither am I.

Lucy: I want us to hang up, and I want to call you back.

James: What does that accomplish?

Lucy: I don't want you to answer your phone. I want to leave you a message.

James: That's cowardly.

Lucy: James! Do not call my bravery into question.

James: Are you still being serious?

Lucy: Yes. I want you to hang up. I'm going to call you back and leave four messages.

James: Four? Holy shit. What do you need to tell me?

Lucy: I need to tell you four things, obviously.

James: You've told me four lies?

Lucy: Stop trying to guess about what I have to say. Let me just tell you.

James: Are you crying?

Lucy: Yeah.

James: Don't cry. It's okay if you bragged yourself up or something. It's not a big deal. I'm tough. You haven't said anything that's worth crying over. Trust me.

Lucy: I think you're going to hate me.

James: Don't be so melodramatic. Of course I'm not going to hate you. I like you.

Lucy: This is hard.

James: Now that you're crying, you're making it hard for me, too. Please. Stop.

Lucy: Stop telling you?

James: No, stop crying.

Lucy: But I feel really bad about this.

James: Just tell me.

Lucy: Hang up, James.

James: Okay. But I can't think of anything you've said that could be this bad.

May 5, 6:27 p.m.
Lucy: I know Beth Howie and Nan.

May 5, 6:29 p.m.
Lucy: I know your brother, Bo.

May 5, 6:31 p.m.
Lucy: CeCe is short for Cecil. She used to date Bo. She was at that party. So was I.

May 5, 6:33 p.m.
Lucy: My name isn't Lucy Villaire.

May 5, 6:40 p.m.
Lucy: I didn't expect you to answer your phone. You probably think that I'm a big liar. But it's not like that. Not totally. My first name really is Lucy. I lied about my last name because . . . Well, I think I'll wait to tell you the reason. I'm sorry, James. I didn't mean to hurt you. Sometimes people do the wrong thing for the right reason. That probably doesn't make much sense to you now. Maybe one day it will. I'll call you later.

May 6

May 7

May 8

May 9

May 10, 7:17 p.m.

Lucy: According to NOAA, it's supposed to be over eighty degrees tomorrow. I think that's a record high. If you ever wanted to get together and go jogging or something, we could do that. Okay. I'm not sure what to do, James. I lied to you. I know I hurt you. Beyond that, I'm not sure what I'm supposed to say. I've been reduced to calling and leaving your voice mail lame messages about the weather. I better go.

May 10, 8:20 p.m.

Lucy: I should have said I'm sorry. That's something I forgot to say in my earlier message. I really didn't mean to lie to you. I tell a lot of people who I don't anticipate having lasting relationships with that my last name is Villaire. Because sometimes when I say my real name, they want to talk to me about something that I don't want to talk about. I'm sort of famous. Not because I'm a movie star or anything like that. I'm famous in a bad way. I mean, people know me because of something bad that happened to me. It was a few years ago. It made it into the national news. I just don't like talking about it. And by the way, when I told you my last name was Villaire, we weren't really involved yet. You were somebody I'd accidentally called on the phone. So don't hate me. Because that wouldn't be fair. Also, don't forget to tell your mom happy Mother's Day tomorrow.

May 14, 5:09 p.m.
Lucy: I'm going to tell you how I know Beth Howie. Okay. I first met Beth Howie in kindergarten. She sat in front of me. She played with her hair a lot and used to hum theme songs from television shows I'd never seen. I can remember that she liked to wear ponytails. She also used to eat her eraser rubbings. I never really clicked with her. My best friend in kindergarten was Samantha York. I don't know who Beth Howie's best friend was. She used to spend a lot of time with the class rabbit. Okay. So it's not like I hid some big secret friendship with Beth Howie from you. I knew her a long time ago. She was sort of a geek. Sounds like she grew out of it. Unless the two of you used to eat eraser rubbings together and clock a lot of time with rabbits. I'll call you again later.

May 15, 8:02 p.m.

Lucy: So today I'm going to tell you how I know Nan. She and I were in second grade together. I have to be honest. I didn't like her very much. She was sort of a tease. Even with the teacher. I know that sounds gross. But she was always trying to get Mr. Pinter's attention. Also, she used to wear skirts a lot, and in second grade that's sort of weird to me. I caught her cheating on a test once. It was a geography test. We were labeling the seven continents and I saw her looking at my paper. I covered up my Antarctica with my hand. And she pinched me on the arm and said I wasn't good at sharing. I stomped on her shoe and she screamed. I ended up having to miss recess. I was never a very big fan of Nan's. Also, her name is Nanette. She started going by Nan in third grade. I moved pretty soon after that, from Burlington to Montpelier, and I never kept in touch with her. So, that's how I know Nan. She wasn't the most sensitive person on the planet. I'm not surprised that you had to break up with her. Or that she started dating your best friend. Hey, one of these days you should answer your phone. Because it would be nice to talk to you again. Seriously.

May 16, 11:28 p.m.

Lucy: You're probably expecting me to leave you a message about Cecil and the party and how I know Bo. But if I do that, I'll also have to tell you about the awful thing that happened to me, and I don't think that's the sort of thing a person should leave on another person's voice mail. Okay. I guess I can tell you this: I only met Bo a couple of times when he and Cecil were hanging out. They weren't really dating. I mean, they just weren't. He was really intense. But I know him another way too. He wrote me a letter when I was in the third grade. I still have it. I think he's a very nice person. I felt really bad when I found out that he had such serious problems. He seems nice. I hope everything works out with him. Bye.

May 17, 9:12 a.m.
Lucy: Hi, James, today is Armed Forces Day. I know this because it says so on my calendar. But I don't know any traditions associated with Armed Forces Day. Do you? Okay. I'll be away tomorrow. My parents and I are leaving for Maine this afternoon. We're taking a tour of Bowdoin. I think that's where they want me to go. Because it's small. And my parents equate small with safe. Which is stupid, because sometimes bombs are small. And poison capsules. And deadly bacteria. And scorpions. Anyway, I worry that I'm not going to like it there. They keep using the words "cozy," "nourishing," and "comfortable." It sort of sounds like they're describing how I feel about waffles. And should

going to college be like eating waffles? Okay. I won't call you tomorrow. But I'll call you Monday. And I'm going to list all the things that I like about you. Because I think if I flatter you enough, you might forgive me. And answer your phone. Listen, I didn't lie to you because I'm a mean person. It's hard for me to be totally honest, because that means that I have to say things that make me feel vulnerable. And sad. And I didn't want to feel those things with you. I wanted to feel happy. Is that so wrong?

May 17, sent 10:10 p.m.
  Lucy: I miss you.

May 18, 2:35 p.m.
  Lucy: I am calling you from the south side of the quad outside Hubbard Hall. If I sound weird, it's because I'm whispering. And crouching behind a bush. There is no way that I can go to school here. It's so small. It would be like going to college inside a coat pocket. It's *that* small. I've thought about what you said about how I'm like a tortoise. How I might miss stuff. You're right. I don't want to miss stuff. For college, I want the "big" experience. I want to be near a city. I mean, this place is twenty-five miles from Portland. And a hundred and twenty miles from Boston. Seriously. I've already spent the best years of my

life living in Montpelier. No. Wait. *East* Montpelier. I want a new existence. I'm ready to blow the lid off my life. I know the world isn't always safe. But you can't stick to eating waffles forever. It can't be done. It's not supposed to happen. Seriously. I'm ready for omelets. And sausages. And breakfast burritos. Thanks for helping me see this. Wow. I bet this message sounds really weird. Sorry. I've been eating sugar all day. I'll call you back later when I'm less wired. Or you could always call me back. I'd like that.

May 18, 9:51 p.m.

Lucy: I know. Two messages in one day. I must sound so desperate. James, I want you to know that if you call me, I'll tell you everything. I'm ready to talk to you and be really honest. Also, the awful thing that happened to me isn't just about me. It's about my sister. Her name is Kathryn. I tell people I'm an only child because Kathryn isn't around anymore. It's a sad story. And it doesn't even have an ending.

May 19, 6:42 a.m.

James: Lucy, I just got your message from last night. I had my phone turned off. I'm ready to talk to you, too. I'm sorry to hear about Kathryn. Lucy, I'm not as mad as I was. I'm ready for you to explain things to me. I think I know who you are.

May 19, 8:12 p.m.

Lucy: I'm scared to talk to you.

James: Don't be.

Lucy: But we haven't talked in a really long time and now things feel so weird.

James: You haven't changed at all. It's only been a couple of weeks and things don't feel that weird.

Lucy: Okay. Um, do you want me to tell you how I know Bo?

James: You told me. He dated CeCe and he wrote you a letter.

Lucy: He and Cecil only went out once. In a group. And he wasn't supposed to be at the party in Waterbury. He crashed it. And he ended up getting kicked out. No other college kids were there.

James: I don't blame CeCe for what Bo did. I got over that before I even knew that Cecil was CeCe.

Lucy: Do you want me to tell you the whole story?

James: Only tell me what you want to.

Lucy: Okay. There's not even a tiny piece of it that's happy.

James: Say it.

Lucy: I'm trying to figure out where to start.

James: Lucy, I'm your friend. Tell me.

Lucy: Here goes. My sister Kathryn, if she were here, she would be twenty-one. Almost twenty-two. She's been missing for eight years. I was with her when she was taken. Or disappeared. Or whatever happened. I mean, I was sort of with her. She packed a picnic lunch for us. We were at Rosemary Park in Burlington. When all this happened, my family still lived in Burlington. We hadn't moved yet. That happened after Kathryn went missing. After all the reporters on the lawn. The hundreds of volunteers. The attention was painful. I hated it. It was like a circus. All these people wanting to watch us and ask us questions. Some because they wanted to help. But others just to sell papers and magazines. It was sick. Okay. I'm skipping around. Back to the picnic. After we finished eating, Kathryn went to use the bathroom. I closed my eyes. I can remember the sun. It was warm and I was so tired. Kathryn had made brownies for dessert. I'd eaten two. My mouth felt sweet. Every time I eat chocolate now, I think of this moment. Okay. I don't remember falling asleep. And I don't know how long I slept. When I woke up, the sky was cloudy and dark. It was about to rain. I called out for Kathryn. But she didn't come. I went to the bathrooms. She wasn't there. I was eight years old when it happened. I should have gone to somebody's house and told them to call 911. But I was so sure that she would come back. I went and sat and waited for her. The clouds broke open and rain poured down. Our neighbor, Mrs. Wong, drove by and saw me and tried to get me to get inside her car. But I wouldn't. Because if I went, I was sure Kathryn would come back and she'd think I'd left her. I didn't want her to think that. I couldn't just abandon her. It had been my idea to go to the park in the first place. It was so awful. I thought they'd find her. I thought maybe she had hurt herself and fallen into something she couldn't get out of. Or maybe she'd hit her head. Or maybe somebody was holding her hostage and she was trying to escape. For a long time, every time the phone rang, I was so sure it would be her. It's hard to believe that a person can just disappear like that. But she did. She's gone.

James: Oh my god. I knew it. You're Lucy Kimble. I remember when this happened. Bo and I were at Rosemary Park that same day.

Lucy: I know. I know. That's what his letter was about. I got it, like, three weeks after Kathryn disappeared. He wrote to me about how he'd seen us there, playing Frisbee. And how sorry he was that she was missing. He talked about what a nice person she was. How she'd offered him a brownie. He'd only met her once, for just a minute or two, but it was like he had been able to understand her and figure out exactly who she was. And that made me feel better, because it made me feel that even though Kathryn wasn't around, all the people she'd met still carried around memories of her. So she might have been missing, but she wasn't erased. Bo's letter really helped. I liked how he talked about how happy Kathryn looked that day. When I think of her, that's how I remember her. Laughing. Smiling. Running through the grass.

James: It's okay that you told me that your last name was Villaire.

Lucy: I tell a lot of people that. Because when I say that my name is Lucy Kimble, people usually ask if I'm the

Lucy Kimble from the news. And that's not how I want people to think of me. I don't want my whole life to be defined by this one thing. A tragedy.

James: I can totally understand that.

Lucy: And I don't like thinking that people know such personal stuff about me. I mean, it's not fair. They're strangers to me. The balance is off. When I say that my name is Villaire, it makes things balanced. Because we're both strangers to each other. That's how it should be.

James: I think I understand.

Lucy: Good.

James: I'm so sorry.

Lucy: That's not what I want to hear. I don't want people to feel sorry for me.

James: I'm not sorry for you. I'm sorry that this happened to you. There's a difference.

Lucy: Yeah. Okay.

James: Lucy, I think we should meet.

Lucy: Paris's eggs should be hatching any day.

James: We don't have to wait for that.

Lucy: But if we rush our meeting, then it won't be like a movie anymore.

James: Actually, this is completely like a movie already.

Lucy: But I feel like there's still stuff I should tell you.

James: You can tell me anything else you want.

Lucy: Do you want to know what I told the plaque maker?

James: Yeah.

Lucy: It's sort of what I told you. But with some stuff added. I said that I was Lucy Kimble and that my sister was Kathryn and that after she vanished and my parents moved us to Montpelier, I planted a dogwood in her memory.

So even if I couldn't watch Kathryn grow up, I could sort of keep track of the tree. I realize that the symbolism is strained, and that the tree doesn't replace Kathryn, and that a person and a tree don't grow at the same rate, but when I was eight, it seemed like a solution in some way.

James: I think that makes sense.

Lucy: Well, when somebody disappears and you don't have a body, you don't have a funeral. There's no death date. So the plaque was going to have her name and her birth date and death date, the day she vanished, so that it would feel more final. I was going to put it at the tree's base. It was something I wanted to do before I went to college.

James: That's so sad. Is there anything I can do to make you feel better?

Lucy: Talking to you makes me feel better.

James: Even after we meet, we can still talk on the phone.

Lucy: That's a weird thing to say. You thought we'd stop talking on the phone after we met?

James: No. I mean, I don't know. Nothing has to change is all that I'm saying. We can see each other and talk on the phone.

Lucy: Okay.

James: Okay.

May 20, 6:19 a.m.
James: How are you?

Lucy: Tired.

James: Are you feeling okay?

Lucy: Don't do this. I hate it when I tell people my story and then they become hypersensitive to my feelings.

James: I wouldn't say that I'm being hypersensitive.

Lucy: Just be normal.

James: Okay. So are you wearing a skirt today?

Lucy: Now that's the James I know and love.

James: Wow.

Lucy: That's just a saying. It doesn't really mean that I love you. Please don't get weirded out. I'm never at my best in the mornings. I'm way too spontaneous.

James: I never noticed that.

Lucy: It's one of the things I was trying to hide.

James: You don't have to hide anything with me. I'm not a judgmental person.

Lucy: I know. You've done a good job not judging me thus far. Hey, I've got great news! CeCe thinks that Paris's eggs will hatch in the next couple of days. What are you doing tomorrow and the day after that and the day after that?

James: I guess I'll be waiting by my phone.

Lucy: I'll try to make it worth your while.

James: I like the sound of that.

Lucy: So are you going to call me Lucy Kimble or Lucy Villaire?

James: I'm probably just going to call you Lucy.

Lucy: But what if we get into a situation where you have to use my last name?

James: What do you want me to say?

Lucy: You can tell your parents that my name is Kimble. And your friends. But not random people.

James: Can we define "random people"?

Lucy: You know. The postal carrier. Waitresses. Door-to-door salespeople. Ice-cream-truck drivers. Lifeguards. Et cetera.

James: You're a goof.

Lucy: Takes one to know one.

James: Hey, can you hear that?

Lucy: Yeah. Did you get a cat? Is it in heat?

James: No. It's my grandmother. She liked singing along to the radio in the car so much, I bought her a kara-oke machine. And she uses it all the time.

Lucy: It sounds like she's singing a rap song.

James: It's a song about Detroit. I got her a bunch of songs about Michigan. I bought this one as a joke, but it's turned out to be one of her favorites.

Lucy: What is it?

James: It's by K-Deezy. Do you know him? The song is "In My Hood." He's a big deal in Detroit.

Lucy: Does your grandma usually like rap music?

James: No. Just this song. I mean, there are a couple by Jay-Z that she likes too. But I'm not sure she'd heard them until now. Maybe she had.

Lucy: What you've done for her is sweet.

James: Helping her rap before seven o'clock in the morning?

Lucy: Yeah. She sounds very happy.

James: I think she's doing really good.

Lucy: What's she singing now?

James: Hard to tell. I think something by Beyoncé.

Lucy: Which song? After Greg and I broke up, I played a lot of her music. I think she's soulful.

James: That's right. Good old Greg Tandy. So what did happen between you two?

Lucy: Well, it's a serious story. It involves track.

James: You and track. I never knew running could be such a serious issue in anybody's life.

Lucy: Do you want to tease me about it or do you want me to talk about it?

James: Can't I have both?

Lucy: I'll call you later and we can talk. It's a sad story.

James: Track is a sad story?

Lucy: It really is.

James: Call me any time you want and tell me all about it. You can even call me at lunch.

Lucy: I can't. CeCe and I have to talk at lunch.

James: Did you ever tell her what happened with Bo?

Lucy: No. It didn't feel like my story.

James: Most people would have told that story.

Lucy: I understand what stories can do. You may have told me, but I didn't think you wanted me to tell other people.

James: Thanks, Lucy. So what are you going to talk about with CeCe at lunch?

Lucy: Taylor Conk.

James: Is that her boyfriend?

Lucy: She's hoping.

James: I've never heard of him.

Lucy: He's not an athlete.

James: I'm friends with people who aren't athletes.

Lucy: He plays the viola.

James: Oh.

Lucy: He's super nice.

James: I don't think I've ever met anybody who played the viola.

Lucy: Maybe we could go on a double date and you could hang out with him.

James: I want to go on a bunch of single dates first.

Lucy: I bet you do.

James: What do you mean by that?

Lucy: I don't really know.

James: You are so corny.

Lucy: James, it's how I roll.

May 20, 11:45 a.m.

James: Hey, Lucy. I just ran into Nan. One thing I never told you about Nan was that I once asked her if Nan was short for Nancy. And she said, "No. My name isn't short for anything. It's just Nan." And so when I ran into her, like, five minutes ago, I asked her, "Hey, Nan, I met somebody who said that your full name is Nanette. Is that true?" And she pinched me on the chest, right above my nipple, and said, "Nobody calls me that anymore. Nobody." She didn't pinch me hard. It was more like a grab. But it made me like her a whole lot less. I get why you didn't tell me the truth about your name. There was a sad story attached to it and we didn't know each other well enough to go there. But Nan. I dated Nan for seven months. And she lied to me about her name the whole time. For no good reason. It's weird how two people can tell the same lie, but the effect of that lie can be totally different. I mean, your lie made me like you more. Isn't that weird?

May 20, 12:08 p.m.

Lucy: What did you eat for lunch? You're thinking way too hard. Seriously. And I can't believe that Nan pinched you. It's like she hasn't changed since second grade at all! And what's with grabbing your nipple? And what's with you telling me that she grabbed your nipple? You know, sometimes too much anatomical precision freaks me out.

May 20, 3:24 p.m.

James: Where are you? And it's disappointing to hear that I can't talk about my nipples. They're interesting.

May 20, 6:18 p.m.

Lucy: When you tell me that your nipples are interesting, it makes me feel like they're shaped wrong. Are they? Okay. I am headed to Sarducci's for dinner with CeCe and Taylor. This is major progress for CeCe. She's thrilled. It's just going to be the three of us. We'll probably eat pizza. Actually, I like the penne pugliese. It has eggplant in it. And I am a huge fan of eggplant. Okay. I am not planning on staying for the entire dinner. I am going to leave early so that they have some time alone. I'll try to call you. But if I don't, it's because I have homework. It's for psychology. I have to write a letter to myself ten years in the future. I am taking it very seriously. Except that I haven't started yet. I mean, I've been thinking about it all semester, because I knew it was coming. But the actual writing process hasn't begun yet. I hope you and your nipples have a good night.

May 21, 5:12 p.m.

James: Sometimes I feel like you're avoiding me.

Lucy: You've got to be joking.

James: You're right. So how did your letter writing go last night?

Lucy: It was actually really hard.

James: But you said you'd been thinking about it all semester.

Lucy: Yeah. It wasn't that I didn't have things to say. It was hard in other ways.

James: Do you want to talk about it?

Lucy: Okay.

James: When are you going to start talking about it?

Lucy: Right now. Geez. It's like you don't even let me breathe.

James: Sometimes you wait almost five or six seconds.

Lucy: I'm b-r-e-a-t-h-i-n-g.

James: I guess I'm talented in that I can talk and breathe at the same time.

Lucy: Okay, okay, okay. It was hard for me to write that letter, because I have to think of the future, and when I think of the future, I have to imagine it without Kathryn. And, even after all these years, that's still sad to me. Because I'd rather imagine her in it.

James: Do you think it will always be hard?

Lucy: Yeah. I mean, there's all these milestones in life. High school graduation. College. Marriage. You know. The important stuff. For her and for me.

James: Do you think the saying is true, that this will get better with time?

Lucy: The pain isn't sharp like it was when she first disappeared. But there's this specific sadness, sort of like a loneliness, that has a way of creeping into my life. I miss Kathryn. And I'll always miss Kathryn.

James: I have a question, but I don't know if it's appropriate.

Lucy: You want to ask an inappropriate question about my missing sister?

James: I don't *know* whether or not it's inappropriate.

Lucy: What is it?

James: When you think about her, do you ever wonder what exactly happened to her?

Lucy: Like who took her?

James: Yeah.

Lucy: Not anymore. I mean, I used to. I'd go to this place and it's all I'd think about. Like I was stuck in these long daydreams. They were frightening and made me feel miserable. Now I try to focus on her life. She was happy.

James: I think I'd be obsessed with it.

Lucy: I've had to put it down. It's too much. For a long time, I saw a therapist every week.

James: You don't anymore?

Lucy: Not right now. Maybe I'll see somebody later. Right now I'm doing okay. This is hard to explain, but even though Kathryn's so absent, she's still sort of present.

James: Has it always felt that way?

Lucy: It comes and goes. Sometimes I really feel her. Other times there's just this sad emptiness. That's why I try to focus on her life. Because she was a great person. She really was.

James: Do you like the way the letter to your future self turned out?

Lucy: Sure. I ask myself a lot of questions.

James: I thought you were supposed to tell yourself things.

Lucy: Yeah. I don't think I really followed the assignment. I didn't want to tell myself things. I have no clue where I'll be in ten years. I might be living in a foreign country.

James: Like Honduras?

Lucy: I was thinking France.

James: I've never been to Honduras or France.

Lucy: Neither have I. I guess we've both got a lot of living left to do.

James: Lucy, I want to thank you for something.

Lucy: Okay. Thank away.

James: Thanks for making me read Bo's letters.

Lucy: I didn't make you.

James: Without you telling me to, I doubt I would have read them. And they've really helped me understand him. Without them, I probably wouldn't have been able to forgive him.

Lucy: So you've forgiven him? Does this mean you trust him again too?

James: I still need to work on that.

Lucy: Have you ever thought of writing letters to Bo?

James: I'm not ready for that.

Lucy: Oh.

James: Maybe one day.

Lucy: I write letters.

James: I know. To your future self in ten years.

Lucy: No. I write letters that aren't part of an assignment.

James: Really? To who?

Lucy: Kathryn. I do it when something exciting or interesting happens. Actually, that's not true. Sometimes nothing all that interesting has happened and I'll sit down and write her.

James: Like a diary? Except in letters?

Lucy: I guess. When I first started doing this, I used to think: What if Kathryn is one of the stories, one of those rare cases, where somebody finds her? I figured that when Kathryn came home, I could give her these. I could show her how much I missed her, how I was always thinking about her. And when she read them, even though all this time has passed, it would be like she hadn't missed *everything*.

James: That's really sad, Lucy.

Lucy: It helps me.

James: Have you written her any letters lately?

Lucy: Oh yeah. I've been keeping her well informed

about Paris and the eggs. I've also told her a little bit about you.

James: Good things?

Lucy: Pretty good things.

James: Can I ask you another question about this?

Lucy: Yes.

James: If you've given her a death date and you don't think that she's going to read them anymore, why do you still write them?

Lucy: I guess I believe in an afterlife and stuff. I think she still has access to them. In some way. She sees them.

James: Oh.

Lucy: I think I'm through talking tonight.

James: That's good. Because I think I'm through listening.

Lucy: That was so rude!

James: I was joking.

Lucy: Jokes can be rude.

James: You're being way too hard on me.

Lucy: Get used to it.

James: What's next? More nipple insults?

Lucy: You're the one who said they were interesting.

James: They are. I mean, if these nipples could talk . . .

May 22, 6:24 a.m.
James: I can't believe that you didn't pick up. Maybe you're in the shower. I think I should get directions to your house again. So that when the hatching begins, I can zoom right over.

May 22, 6:58 a.m.
Lucy: I can't believe that *you* aren't picking up. You're such a tease. Okay. I'm going to forgive you for losing these directions. I live on Township Road. It's the fourth house. If you pass a barn with the words "Cream Dog,"

you've gone too far. But I bet you remembered that part. You'll know you're getting close when you've left all signs of civilization behind. On a side note, in the background of your last message I could hear your grandma singing. I think it might have been Neil Diamond. My dad listens to him a lot. I didn't know that anybody else did. Hey, when it comes to selecting karaoke songs, I think your grandma has tremendous range.

May 22, 7:03 a.m.

James: Yes, I was in the shower. And, Lucy, I never told you this before, but your directions are terrible. You need to give a person landmarks. Gas stations. Cemeteries. Big gangly trees.

May 22, 7:08 a.m.

Lucy: Are you taking a second shower? Did you have trouble rinsing out your shampoo? Okay. Take the main exit in Montpelier and drive straight until you don't see any landmarks. No gas stations. No cemeteries. No big gangly trees. Then turn left on Township Road. My house is blue. It looks like a triangle. It's the only house on the hill. If you get lost, call me. Oh, and Paris isn't at my house. Paris is at CeCe's. Remember? Anyway, once the hatching starts, you drive here and then we can carpool to CeCe's together.

May 22, 9:39 p.m.

James: You never told me all the things you like about me.

Lucy: What are you talking about?

James: In one of your messages, during one of our no-talk periods, you said that you were going to call me and tell me all the things you liked about me.

Lucy: Are you sure I said that?

James: I still have the message.

Lucy: Are you demanding that I tell you what I like about you right now?

James: Well, I don't like the way the word "demand" sounds. But yes.

Lucy: Okay. Let me think. I am going to limit this to five things I like about you. Is that all right?

James: Five is a good start.

Lucy: The first thing is easy. You're funny. And not in your average way. You're clever-funny and I like that a lot.

James: Go on.

Lucy: Go on about clever-funny or go on to the second thing?

James: Either way.

Lucy: The second thing. I like how you're interested in my life. Even though sometimes I don't like sharing stuff with you. You seem very thoughtful and I like that a lot.

James: Next.

Lucy: Okay. Number three. You're adventurous. You go camping. You play sports. You think tortoises waste their slow-moving lives. I like that. It means that you're willing to live. And you help me want that.

James: That's true. I refuse to be a tortoise.

Lucy: Four. I like that you like your grandma. And that

you drive her around. And bought her a karaoke machine. You seem very sweet. And you seem connected to your family in a real positive way.

James: Thanks.

Lucy: And for five, I guess I like the sound of your voice.

James: That's not very positive. I can't help the sound of my voice. It's biological. It's something that just is.

Lucy: Well, it's pleasant and I like it.

James: Describe how it's pleasant.

Lucy: You're so demanding!

James: You're acting dodgy. Does this mean that my voice is pleasant, yet indescribable?

Lucy: Your voice is kind. And calm. And the sound of it makes me want to trust you.

James: That was a pretty good five.

Lucy: Well, what do you like about me?

James: Hmm. Give me a second. Okay. You're sweet and sharp and interesting and funny and you've got a lot of energy.

Lucy: We only talk on the phone. How do you know whether or not I have a lot of energy?

James: You're enthusiastic about stuff. Plus, you used to run track.

Lucy: But I don't run track anymore.

James: True. True. This seems like a good time to tell me why you don't run track anymore.

Lucy: Okay. But you can't get mad at Greg Tandy.

James: Greg Tandy made you stop running track?

Lucy: Sort of.

James: What did he do?

Lucy: Okay. That part comes later. First, let me explain my running anxieties.

James: Running makes you feel anxious?

Lucy: James! I can understand why you used to get mad when I jumped in and interrupted your stories. It's very annoying. Stop acting like me.

James: Fair enough.

Lucy: When I ran, I wanted to be the fastest. The best. The person that stunned everybody because I had this incredible, never-ending speed. But the way I got that speed was by imagining horrible things.

James: Like you were being chased?

Lucy: Exactly. I pictured myself being chased by a man. He didn't have a face. He was sort of like a shadow. I used to pretend that this was the person who took Kathryn. And he was after me. I know this sounds stupid. But the fear knocked all sorts of things loose inside of me. And when I did this, when I imagined this man, my adrenaline rushed through me and I always won every race.

James: Did this feel good or bad?

Lucy: It felt good at first, but then it quickly turned into a bad feeling. I hated to think that I was using Kathryn and this thing that had happened to her to gain some sort of attention. I was really disappointed in myself. I felt ashamed.

James: Could you run without imagining this man?

Lucy: Yes, but when I did that, I never won.

James: How does Greg Tandy factor into this equation?

Lucy: Well, for a long time, I never told anybody about this. Because I was ashamed. When I finally told Greg, he seemed to think it was a good strategy. And the few times I lost, when I didn't imagine myself being chased, he got really angry with me. He'd say things like "You're throwing away your advantage." And "It gives you an edge; you'd be stupid not to use it."

James: What an asshole.

Lucy: He loves winning. He's addicted to it. You saw

how he played basketball. Losing wasn't an option. Well, one day I realized that running track made me miserable. It just hit me. And I decided to quit. Greg was furious. He told me that I was a coward. And that made me totally flip. I couldn't believe he'd said that to me. So I slapped him. I know. I shouldn't have done that. But it was like a reflex. What he said hurt me so deeply that some sort of self-defense mechanism kicked in and I clapped my hand right across his cheek.

James: Good for you.

Lucy: No. I shouldn't have slapped him. Hitting other people isn't the way to solve your problems.

James: It seems to have solved this one.

Lucy: Well, it sort of did. Because he broke up with me. Right there. His cheek started glowing pink and he touched it in disbelief. And he said, "I can't believe a girl just hit me." And I said, "That wasn't a hit. It was a slap." And he said, "I'm out of here, Lucy. You've got serious emotional problems." And I thought about yelling, "I'm sorry." But I didn't. I watched him go. And I felt completely miserable for about a week. And sort of miserable for a month. But then I started feeling less and less miserable about it. And now I don't miss him at all.

James: That's good. He's a jerk.

Lucy: I guess. I don't even care. He is what he is. And he's not a part of my life anymore.

James: So, do you miss running at all? Would you ever want to go jogging?

Lucy: I'd love to go jogging with the right partner.

James: Do you want to go jogging tomorrow after school? It's supposed to be a sunny day. I checked NOAA.

Lucy: I thought we were waiting for Paris's eggs to hatch before we met.

James: Lucy, waiting is stupid.

Lucy: Yeah. I agree. So, um, do you want to meet tomorrow?

James: I do.

Lucy: But what if it changes things?

James: Stop saying that. You're not a tortoise anymore, remember?

Lucy: But what if, James, what if?

James: I won't let anything change. Lucy, you're one of my best friends. You've really helped me with Bo. And my feelings. We're only going to become better friends.

Lucy: That was a sweet thing to say.

James: Well, I'm a sweet guy. You said so yourself.

Lucy: What time tomorrow?

James: What are you doing at four o'clock?

Lucy: I think I'm meeting James Rusher.

James: Cool.

Lucy: This is so freaky.

James: It's not freaky.

Lucy: It's something.

James: It's all good.

May 23, 6:19 a.m.
James: I was wondering if I should bring anything today. For you or for Paris. Or maybe even CeCe or Santiago. It seems like one parakeet is completely overshadowing the other. That can't be good for a keet's self-esteem.

May 23, 6:34 a.m.
Lucy: You need to get a waterproof phone, so I can call you when you're in the shower. Because that seems to be the place I miss you most. Okay. It's thoughtful of you to want to bring something. I know we talked about giving each other surprises, but you don't need to do that. Seriously. You only need to bring yourself.

May 23, 7:00 a.m.
James: You are the first girl who ever said that she

missed me when I was in the shower. Lucy, Lucy, Lucy. I wonder if you jog half as good as you flirt.

May 23, 3:38 p.m.

Lucy: Come now! Come now! The eggs are hatching.

James: I'm almost to your house.

Lucy: Wow. You're early.

James: Only by, like, ten minutes.

Lucy: So you're telling me that you're ten minutes away?

James: You're quick.

Lucy: Don't tease me. I'm feeling way too fragile for that.

James: What's wrong?

Lucy: I'm nervous.

James: About Paris?

Lucy: About you!

James: There's no reason to be nervous about me. We've covered this already. I'm totally great. You've got a long list to back it up.

Lucy: I know. It's just. Oh my god. We're going to meet.

James: That's a good thing.

Lucy: Yeah. Yeah.

James: Hey, I think I see your house.

Lucy: You do? That didn't take ten minutes. Are you sure you see *my* house?

James: Well, I'm in the middle of nowhere. I haven't seen a landmark or sign of civilization for miles. The house I'm looking at is the fourth one on the left and it's blue. And also shaped like a triangle.

Lucy: Are you driving a green car?

James: Yep.

Lucy: I can see you, too!

James: Wow. Your house is big.

Lucy: James, before we meet, I need to tell you something.

James: You've got something else to tell me?

Lucy: It's about my hair.

James: Are you really a baldy?

Lucy: No. Nothing that dramatic.

James: That's a relief.

Lucy: I dye my hair.

James: What color? Green?

Lucy: Red. But my natural color is brown.

James: I don't care what color your hair is.

Lucy: I bet you would if it really was green.

James: Your car must be an all-wheel drive. I mean, your driveway has a steep grade.

Lucy: I told you. I live on a hill.

James: I see that. Hey, is that your dogwood?

Lucy: Yes, that's it. Oh my god. You're parking!

James: Yes. It's something I often do after I arrive somewhere by car.

Lucy: You're getting out of your car. You've got a bag. Did you bring something for Paris?

James: No, they're churros. For you. Where are you?

Lucy: Up here. In my window. Hey, where are you going?

James: I'm taking a look at your tree. It's growing buds. It'll probably blossom in a few weeks.

Lucy: The plaque arrived today. Crazy timing, right?

James: That's amazing.

Lucy: Do you see a good place where I should attach it? Maybe the south side of the base? Or maybe the west side? It's sunnier.

James: I didn't drive all the way down to East Montpelier with a sack of churros to inspect the shade of your dogwood.

Lucy: Yeah. You're right. I'll figure it out.

James: Do you want me to ring the doorbell? Or are you going to come down?

Lucy: Why don't you come to my window? I can't totally see you yet.

James: Maybe it's because you're two stories above me.

Lucy: Oh, I can see you now. Oh my god. It's you! It's you! I can see your head. And your face. You're exactly what I expected.

James: Lucy, why are we still talking on the phone?

LOST IT

I didn't start out my junior year of high school planning to lose my virginity to Benjamin Easter—a senior—at his parents' cabin in Island Park underneath a sloppily patched, unseaworthy, upside-down canoe. Up to that point in my life, I'd been somewhat of a prude who'd avoided the outdoors, especially the wilderness, for the sole purpose that I didn't want to be eaten alive.

I'm from Idaho. The true West. And if there's a beast indigenous to North America that can kill you, it probably lives here. My whole life, well-meaning people have tried to alleviate my fear of unpredictable, toothy carnivores.

But I was never fooled by the pamphlets handed to me by

tan-capped park rangers during the seven-day camping trip that my parents forced upon me every summer. The tourist literature wanted you to believe that you were safe as long as you hung your food in a tree and didn't try to snap pictures of the buffalo within goring distance. Seriously, when in the presence of a buffalo, isn't *any* distance within goring distance?

And they expect intelligent people to believe that a bear can't smell menstrual blood? A bear's nose is more sensitive than a dog's. Every Westerner knows that. In my opinion, if you're having your period and you're stupid enough to pitch a tent in Yellowstone Park, you're either crazy or suicidal. Maybe both.

It's clear why losing my virginity outdoors, in the wilderness, with Benjamin Easter should be taken as an enormous shock. I could have been eaten by a mountain lion, mauled by a grizzly bear, or (thanks to some people my father refers to as "troublemaking tree huggers") torn to pieces by a pack of recently relocated gray wolves.

Of course, I wasn't. To be completely honest, I may be overstating the actual risk that was involved. It happened in December. The bears were all hibernating. And the event didn't end up taking that long. Plus, like I already said, we were hidden underneath a canoe.

But the fact that I lost it in a waterproof sleeping bag on top of a patch of frozen dirt with Benjamin Easter is something that I'm still coming to terms with.

I can't believe it. Even though I've had several days to process the event. I let a boy see me completely naked, and by this I mean braless and without my underpants. I let a boy I'd known for less than four months bear witness to the fact that my right breast was slightly smaller than my left one. And would I do it again?

We did do it again. After the canoe, in the days that followed, we did it two more times. I remember them well. Honestly, I remember them *very* well. Each moment is etched into my mind like a petroglyph. After the third and final time, I watched as he rolled his body away from mine. With my ring finger, I tussled his curly brown hair. Then, I fell asleep. When I woke up, Ben was dressed again, kissing me good-bye. I find myself returning to this moment often. Like it's frozen in time. Sadly, you can't actually freeze time.

Last night, Ben told me, "You're acting outrageous." He said this while inserting a wooden spoon into the elbow-end of my plaster cast. He was trying to rescue the hamster. The hamster had been my idea. I'd just bought it for him. I wanted him to take it to college and always think of me, his broken-armed first love. But the rodent had weaseled its way into my cast. I hadn't realized that hamsters were equipt with burrowing instincts. I also had no idea how to make a boy stay in love with me. Hence, the pet hamster.

It's been hours since I've talked to Ben. Since the hamster

episode. And the argument that followed the hamster episode. That night Ben told me to stop calling him. He was serious. I told him to have a happy New Year. And he hung up on me. The boy I'd lost it with in a sleeping bag in the frozen dirt had left me with nothing but a dial tone.

I swear, the day I woke up and started my junior year of high school, Benjamin Easter wasn't even on my radar. I didn't know a thing about leukemia. And because I was raised by deeply conservative people, who wouldn't let me wear mascara or attend sex education classes at Rocky Mountain High School, I wasn't even aware that I had a hymen or that having sex would break it.

Actually, in the spirit of full disclosure and total honesty, I should mention that my parents only became born-again rather recently, at about the time I hit puberty, following a serious grease fire in the kitchen. Before that, they only ventured to church on major holidays. Hence, my life became much more restricted and we gave up eating deep-fried foods.

The day I started my junior year, I woke up worrying about the size of my feet. Once dressed, looking at myself in my full-length bedroom mirror, they struck me as incredibly long and boatlike. I squished them into a pair of shoes I'd worn in eighth grade, brown suede loafers. They pinched, but gave my feet the illusion of looking regular-size instead of Cadillac-size. Then I noticed a newly risen zit. Of course, under the cover of darkness, it had cowardly erupted in the center of my forehead. I held back my brown bangs and popped it. Then I dabbed the surrounding area with a glob of beige-colored Zit-Be-Gone cream.

I started the first day of my junior year of high school zitless and basically happy. I was sixteen and feeling good. I didn't have any major issues. Okay, that's not entirely true. For weeks I'd been growing increasingly concerned about Zena Crow, my overly dramatic best friend. She'd been going through a rocky stretch and had been talking incessantly about building a bomb. Not a big bomb. Just one that was big enough to blow up a poodle.

READ ON FOR EVEN MORE!

CRIMES OF THE SARAHS

Just like mayonnaise, Raisinets, and milk, every criminal has a shelf life. Either you get caught or you evolve. Much like the amoeba, the other Sarahs and I plan on evolving. Of course, since we're in the middle of a job right now, we're obviously not there yet.

"Should I go?" Sarah B asks.

I view this as a rhetorical question. I'm not the leader. That's Sarah A's position, but she's already inside the store. Sometimes, because I'm the driver, when Sarah A is absent, the other two Sarahs defer to me. Though I don't know why. Among the four of us, I'm the least alpha. I'm not headstrong or decisive or anything. As far as the pecking order, I'm the shortest Sarah. Plus, I struggle with anxiety.

"Give her a few more minutes," Sarah C calls from the backseat.

Had I said something, that would've been my answer too. I always favor inaction over action. Sarah B leans back into the passenger seat and smacks her gum. Then she blows a bubble so big that its circumference eclipses her face. *Pop.* She peels off the pink film and pushes the gum wad back inside her mouth. Bubbles never stick to Sarah B's face, because every minute of her life, her T-zone is aglow with oil. It's what I call a Teflon complexion. Except I don't say that to her actual face. *Pop.*

A fact that sucks: Sarah B breaks out more than any other Sarah. Another fact that sucks: Her oily skin will age better than my dry skin. When she's eighty, her skin will be the least wrinkly of all the Sarahs. That is, if we all live long enough to reach that geriatric benchmark.

"Now?" Sarah B asks.

I shake my head. It's not just that I favor inaction; in the beginning, we learned quickly that it was best to enter our targeted stores one at a time. It's blatantly unfair, but salesclerks absolutely stereotype teenagers. Even a group of presumably innocent, Caucasian-looking, female teens browsing the aisles of a bookstore on a Sunday afternoon can send up a red flag. Agism is alive and well, even here in Kalamazoo.

"Now?" Sarah B asks me again. "I feel like it's time."

I nod. I don't know if it's time, but there's so much tension and perfume overload in the car that I'm getting a headache and it would improve the atmosphere immensely if the apple-scented Sarah B left.

"Remember, take the clerk to the board-book display beneath the huge toad cutout. Ask a lot of questions about Sarah Stewart and David Small. Keep the clerk in one area," Sarah C says. She's leaning forward, wedging herself into the rectangle of open space between the driver's and passenger's seat. Her shiny red hair is so close to my mouth that I think I can taste her conditioner.

Sarah B opens the car and slings her purse strap over her neck. For as long as I can remember, Sarah B has feared being mugged. I guess being a thief lowers your threshold for trust.

"I thought it was a cutout of a lizard," Sarah B says.

"He's a toad," Sarah C says.

"How do you know it's a guy? Is it anatomically correct? Did you inspect its crotch?" She blows another bubble and sucks it back inside her mouth.

"First, he's wearing pants. Second, he's a character from *The Wind in the Willows*. It's a guy toad. Trust us."

Sarah C kicks the back of my seat.

"Yeah, *The Wind in the Willows* is about a male toad," I say.

Sarah B tilts her head and squints at us, like she's thinking really hard. Her soft lips turn downward, which usually means that she's confused.

"I bet some cultures consider lizards to be a form of toads," Sarah B says. "They both have reptile brains." Not everything Sarah B says makes perfect sense.

She slams the car door and enthusiastically walks through the strip mall parking lot, her brown hair bouncing around her tan, bare shoulders. Until last week, Sarah B always wore a Detroit Tigers baseball cap. But after she almost got caught shoving a box of Oreos down her pants at a Sunoco station, Sarah A was adamant that the cap had to go. She claimed that the bill shaded Sarah B's eyes, making her look boyish and deceptive.

Sarah A was the only Sarah who saw it this way. Sarah B has very big boobs. There's nothing boyish going on with that rack. But immediately following the Oreo incident, while we sat around Sarah A's bedroom indulging in our looted booty, Sarah A grabbed the cap right off of Sarah B's head and doused it with lighter fluid. I was really surprised that an incoming high school senior kept lighter fluid in her bedroom. Then, Sarah A ran to her bathroom and torched the hat in the tub. At that point, the cap became a moot point.

But we've all moved on from the flaming cap episode. That's clear as I watch Sarah B bounce right through the front doors of the Barnes & Noble. But what else would I expect? She's a resilient Sarah. We're all resilient Sarahs. So while it may be true that we've reached a criminal level of boredom with our city, to the point where we've considered committing much more serious crimes with actual weapons, we're still a very plucky bunch.

"I'll go in ten," Sarah C calls from the backseat.

She's the only Sarah among us who had to legally change her name. It wasn't the easiest thing to do. She and her parents had to petition the family division of the circuit court and pay almost two hundred dollars. Sarah A made Sarah C bring the paperwork to prove she'd done it. Because if you're going to become part of an elite club, there's got to be some standards. Sarah A was very clear about that. So, our freshman year, Lisa Sarah Cody became Sarah Lisa Cody. A bona fide Sarah. For the most part, she doesn't seem to regret it. But who wouldn't want to be one of us? The benefits are stellar. The Sarahs are popular, crafty, goal-oriented, and have loads of unsupervised time. My parents aren't expecting me home for hours. And when I do show up, it's not like they'll pepper me with probing questions about my afternoon. A few years ago, after I joined the school choir, they assumed I was on a good path in life. I look like a good girl, and around them, I act like a good girl. Which is cool. I may be passive, but I do care what people, especially blood relatives, think about me.

"Hey, don't you ever worry that we'll get caught?" Sarah C asks.

She finger flicks the back of my head. I rub the area and keep my hand there to shield myself from a second flick.

"Are you speaking hypothetically?" I ask.

"No, like right now. Don't you worry some hyperaware clerk will spot us?" Sarah C asks.

"That's not what I was thinking about at all," I say.

"Even if we do get caught, I guess it's not a huge deal because we're minors. We'd probably be sentenced to make restitution and pick up roadside trash. But after we turn eighteen, we might want to rethink this lifestyle."

"Lifestyle?" I try to glance at her in the rearview mirror, but her head is tucked down. "This is more than a lifestyle. It's who we are. We're the Sarahs."

"Yeah, I know, but once we're eighteen, once we're in college, we should probably rethink it. I mean, theft is kind of immature. We want. We take. Is it really worth it?"

"Of course it's worth it. Look around. We've got a close circle of friends and a ton of free crap."

Sarah C leans forward again. This time she angles her body so she can face me. I don't look at her.

"But doesn't all the free crap ever weigh on your conscience?" she asks.

"My what?"

Sarah C lowers her voice to a whisper.

"Sometimes, I picture myself handcuffed. Actually, I imagine all four of us in handcuffs, being trotted out to a squad car, the lights flashing, broadcasting our guilt to everybody driving by."

Sarah C mimics a siren by emitting a *wha wha* sound. Then she puts her hand over her mouth to dim the noise.

I'm so shaken up her pessimistic outpouring that my jaw drops open. A light breeze blows into the pocket of my mouth.

She stops the siren sound.

"It's not about the theft," I say. At least that's what Sarah A always says. "It's about the bond. The sisterhood."

"We could get tattoos."

This idea makes me frown. I'm not sure that I want a tattoo. And because Sarah C has the highest GPA out of all the Sarahs and also scored 2300 on the SAT, sometimes her suggestions carry weight.

"Why would we want to put identifying markers on our bodies?" I ask.

"Good point," Sarah C says. "In a lineup we'd be so screwed."

"A lineup?" I ask.

"Yeah, don't you watch cop shows?" Sarah C asks.

"You have time to watch cop shows?" I ask.

I'm surprised to hear this because being a Sarah takes up all my free time.

"This probably isn't the best time to ponder cop shows," Sarah C say. "The criminals usually get locked up."

"Yeah," I say. "Let's ponder something positive."

There's a long silence.

"Can't you think of anything positive?" I ask.

"Stealing stuff all the time is a lot like driving a race car," Sarah C says. "Drivers are warned not to look at the wall when they're losing control, because you tend to steer yourself toward what you're looking at. For criminals that's a very appropriate life metaphor: In order to avoid colliding with the cops, don't think about them."

"I never think about the police," I say. Neither the topic of law enforcement or car crashes strike me as positive pondering.

"Besides the Sarahs, what do you think about?" Sarah C asks. I don't like her tone; it's accusatory. Or her question; it's a little too insightful.

"I think about life," I say.

Sarah C leans into the backseat again, but this time threads her long legs through the center console. Her sandals reach the gearshift. I get the feeling that she doesn't believe me. She crosses her ankles and I watch her toes curl incredulously against the brown suede pad of her shoes. I feel goaded into elaboration.

"I think about life all the time," I say. "It's like a hallway."

"A hallway?"

"Yeah," I say.

"Like at school?" Sarah C asks.

"Okay, but there's no lockers," I say. "It's just a hallway and there's all these doors. But they're closed. So you've got to decide which ones to open and which ones to walk past. But you never know what you're missing or what you're getting until you've already gotten it," I say.

Sarah C doesn't say anything right away.

"That's a very interior metaphor. I spend a lot of time outdoors. That comparison doesn't really work for me," Sarah C says.

"*My life* is like a hallway," I say.

"That's tragic. I really dig trees," Sarah C says.

I turn and look at Sarah C in the backseat. She's twisting a small section of her red hair around her pointer finger.

"Didn't Sarah A tell you to keep your hair pulled back into a ponytail?" I ask.

"She did, but it makes my neck look so long."

"Aren't swan necks considered attractive?" I ask.

"Maybe. But I like my hair down."

"Sarah C, remember the Oreos," I say.

I turn back to face the front and look out the windshield. I'm thirsty. But I never consume any fluid for at least four hours before a hit. Too much anxiety triggers my pee reflex. I can hear the sound of an elastic band snapping itself into place. Sarah A thinks ponytails look wholesome. She thinks it's the right message to send.

"You've got two more minutes," I say.